Weekly Reader Children's Book Club presents

THE BIG TUSKER

WEEKLY READER
CHILDREN'S BOOK CLUB

This is a registered trademark

THE BIG TUSKER

Arthur Catherall

ILLUSTRATED BY DOUGLAS PHILLIPS

Lothrop, Lee and Shepard Co., New York

Contents

A Boy and His Elephant

IN THE JUNGLE COUNTRY OF NORTHWEST THAILAND THE
new day always started with the crowing of jungle
cocks. After one began others immediately answered
his challenge, until for miles and miles the little
alarm clocks awakened both wilderness and tiny village to life.

In the teak camp the old cook crawled from his
bamboo shelter and, shivering in the chill, hurried
across to his cookhouse to blow his sleeping fire to
bright, sputtering life. While he was doing that the
paijaiks, or chain boys, reluctantly emerged from a
dozen huts. Like the old cook they shivered in the
chill of dawn. Among them was Ba Thet, not yet sixteen, but slim and tall for his age—almost five feet
six. He had a mop of unruly black hair and his clothing was a simple outfit of shirt and shorts. He wore
no shoes and at his belt was a jungle knife, called a
dah.

7

While the other *paijaiks* hovered near the fire waiting to warm their hands, Ba Thet moved off into the canopy of overhanging trees from which cold dew dripped like slow rain.

He was excited. Today was the last day for hauling logs this season. He and his uncle, who was the *oozie*, or rider, of their elephant Poo Koon, had about six logs to clear from the long slope up the valley—logs that had stuck on the slide. After that they would wait for the rains.

Unlike teak logging in Burma, where the elephants were owned by the government, the elephants who hauled teak in upper Thailand were all owned by their *oozies*, or by contractors.

Poo Koon, perhaps the youngest bull elephant working in this valley, was almost owned by Ba Thet's father and his uncle Sing Noi. They had started to buy Poo Koon four years ago, and when Ba Thet and his uncle drew their wages in a few days' time they would be able to pay off the last of the money owing for him. It would be a great day for them. Poo Koon was the biggest tusker in that part of the country, standing nine feet two inches at the shoulder, and Ba Thet was ready to fight any other *paijaik* who dared say otherwise.

It did not cost very much to keep a big bull elephant, even though one of them could eat about six hundred pounds of fodder a day. They found their own food. When they had finished the day's work

8

the elephants were scrubbed in a pool. Then chain fetters were fastened around their forefeet, and they were turned loose to forage in the jungle.

One disadvantage was that they often walked for miles. So every morning their owners had to go out at dawn to look for them and bring them back. Ba Thet thought he knew where Poo Koon would be. Lately he had been eating a lot of bamboo shoots, and the previous day Ba Thet had found him in a patch of tall *kaing* grass. He would probably be there now.

The sun rose before Ba Thet got to the *kaing* grass. As he walked along he twice stopped to listen to the *tong-tong* of elephant bells, but neither elephant was his tusker. Poo Koon wore a hand-carved teak clapper bell, and Ba Thet could recognize its sound quite easily. Every elephant bell had its own peculiar note.

When he reached the *kaing* grass the only sounds came from the insects, buzzing and droning busily now that the sun was warming everything and drying the dew off the grass.

"I know you are here," Ba Thet shouted, chuckling to himself, "and I know why you are silent. You've probably plugged the bell with mud, you rogue, but I can wait."

He began to sing, listening intently all the time, but there was no sound from the tall grass. The only way an elephant could be seen was when he moved. Then the tops of the grass swayed.

9

After seven or eight minutes Ba Thet heard the single *tonk* of a bell, and knew he had been right. Poo Koon was in the *kaing* grass. "I know you are there," Ba Thet shouted. "Come on!" But only the insects moved.

The first lesson Ba Thet had learned from his father was to be patient when dealing with a bull elephant. With a swing of its trunk an angry tusker can knock a man a dozen yards. If it picks him up it can throw him twenty feet into a tree.

Though Ba Thet was hungry, he kept his temper and continued calling Poo Koon until finally, with a muffled *tonk-tonk-tonk* and a waving of the tall grass, the mighty elephant came into view, and stood staring at Ba Thet. If an elephant's eyes can twinkle, then Poo Koon's eyes were twinkling, for Ba Thet had been right about the teak clapper bell. Mud had been stuffed inside so that the clapper could not work properly.

"Being funny, eh?" Ba Thet yelled in pretended anger. "If we weren't in a hurry I'd cane your big backside. Do you think we have all day to waste? We have logs to clear off the hill slope. *Hmit! Hmit!*" (Kneel! Kneel!)

Poo Koon leisurely dragged up a clump of *kaing* grass, knocked the dry earth from the roots, popped the middle of the clump into his big mouth, and slowly sat down, chewing.

"One day you will go too far," Ba Thet warned

him, knocking the mud from the bell. "Do you hear?"
And he drummed on the elephant's forehead. It must
have produced a pleasant sensation, for the big
tusker lifted his trunk and, laying the tip on the boy's
shoulder, began to stroke him gently.

"You are an old fool, you are," Ba Thet said, trying to speak severely. But he drummed again on the big forehead, and Poo Koon made a satisfied gurgling sound deep in his throat.

A minute later the leg hobbles had been unfastened and tossed across the tusker's thick neck. That done, Ba Thet climbed up and, with one leg tucked under him, made himself comfortable behind the broad head.

"Now, let us have no more fooling," he said sternly. "You have been stuffing yourself with *kaing* grass and palm-tree fronds all the night, and I am empty as an old coconut shell. Get a move on." And he scratched behind the bull's right ear with his big toenail.

Poo Koon gave a deep *hurrmp!* and, turning from the *kaing* grass, slithered down a bank and onto the bed of the river, which was the easiest way back to camp.

Most of the other teak-dragging elephants were already assembled at the camp when Ba Thet and Poo Koon arrived. There was an atmosphere of happiness around the cook's shack this morning. The hard work of the season was almost ended. Except for Poo Koon, who would be clearing logs from the slide, the elephants would be working in the river-bed, tidying up piles of teak logs that were waiting for the river to rise and wash them downstream. Once in the main river, they would float for hundreds of miles to the sawmills near Bangkok.

In a week's time the contractors and those lucky men who owned their own elephants would get their money. They would put their thumbprint on a pay sheet as a signature, and receive a gleaming heap of shiny ticals, worth about a quarter each. For some months, then, they would rest. While the elephants grew fat on the lush growth that followed the monsoon rains, their owners would be back in their own villages with their families.

Now Poo Koon went to stand with the other elephants, and Ba Thet joined the queue at the cook's shack. Here each *paijaik* and *oozie* picked up a big glossy leaf and, holding it like a plate, with a hand in the center, received a big ladle full of steaming rice, then a smaller scoop of tongue-burning spices.

There were coconut shells nearby and a big drum full of water. Each diner filled his coconut shell with water, then walked off to have his breakfast. No one used a knife or fork but ate with his fingers, squeezing the rice into a ball, dipping it into the spices, then popping it into his mouth. The water in the coconut shell they used for cleaning their fingers when they had finished eating.

Bill Johnson, the teak wallah, or head of the camp, inspected the elephants before work began. Then he issued his orders for the day. He finished with a warning, "I don't want any logs left lying where they can't be floated into the main stream when the river rises. You've all seen the flame-of-the-forest trees.

13

They bloomed yesterday; that means the rains can be here within twenty-four hours. If we get a good rise of river water, you could all be paid off and home in a week."

Everyone smiled and nodded at that. Then the *oozies* climbed onto their elephants, and within five minutes the big dark-gray beasts were gone.

Only one of them turned north—Poo Koon. Because he was the biggest, and said to be the strongest, he had the task of climbing the steep slope and loosening the few logs that had got stuck on the valley side. A special bonus was paid for such work, because it was dangerous. Only the strongest and most agile tuskers were chosen to do it.

Ba Thet and his uncle were in high good humor as they left the camp with Poo Koon, who had chains and dragging wires across his back. Ba Thet walked ahead of the elephant, a sharp, narrow-headed ax in his right hand. He used the ax to chop holes in logs through which to thread the hauling chains, although the logs on the slide ought to have such holes already cut. Still, the ax was a *paijaik's* tool, almost like a badge of office.

Away to the north there was a haziness about the sky, and it was a slightly deeper blue. Ba Thet's uncle called to his nephew, "See the sky ahead? The rains will come tomorrow. The clouds are forming up there."

"If they came today I would be pleased," Ba Thet

14

called back. "The sooner we finish, the sooner we collect our money, and we can pay the debt we owe on our elephant."

"*Our* elephant?" Sing Noi chuckled. "I thought it was my brother, thy father, who was partner with me. Hast grown to be a man during the last night?"

Ba Thet looked back and grinned. Next to his father he liked Sing Noi better than anyone. His uncle had taught him much about elephants that other *paijaiks* did not yet know. He had even allowed Ba Thet to work Poo Koon when they were far away from where Bill Johnson could see.

"When you and my father are old men, Uncle," Ba Thet shouted, "then I shall buy Poo Koon from you. He will be my eleph—"

Suddenly he stopped, for without even a whisper of sound two men had stepped out from a clump of bushes and had barred the way.

Sing Noi halted the big tusker by scratching him behind one ear. He and Ba Thet looked at the two men, noting their black clothing and the fact that one carried a long sword and the other a rifle. They were, Ba Thet guessed, Mooser villagers, though what they were doing in this part of Thailand he could not imagine.

Sing Noi gave them a greeting, smiling in friend-liest fashion. It was always a pleasure to meet strangers, for then one could get news of what was happening in distant parts of the country. In the

Keng Oom Valley there were no newspapers and no radios. News came only with travelers passing through.

"That is a wonderful bull elephant, friend," said the man with the rifle. "Does it belong to the white man who runs the teak-logging camp?"

"It belongs to this boy's father and me," Sing Noi said proudly. "It is the biggest and strongest young bull elephant anywhere in the country."

"I could find an hour's work for him," said the man with the rifle. Then he added quickly, "There would be payment of twenty ticals for the task, and all I need besides is that you keep silent about the work you did."

Ba Thet looked up at his uncle anxiously. He did not like this kind of talk and he did not like the rifle. In the past there had been so many armed thieves that now only policemen, hunters, and teak wallahs were allowed to carry arms.

Sing Noi had been smiling pleasantly at the mention of twenty ticals, but the suggestion that he must not talk wiped the smile from his lips. "I am sorry," he said, gravely shaking his head, "but I am contracted to the white man, and there is work to do that cannot wait. If you look beyond the valley you will see that the monsoon clouds are blowing this way. The river may be flooded tomorrow."

"Then if you will not help us for pay," said the leader of the Mooser men, lifting his rifle and pointing it at Poo Koon's forehead, "you will help for nothing—and still say nothing. If you do speak, when this work is done, be sure we will seek you out and kill you."

The second man unsheathed his sword and, taking Ba Thet by the arm, moved him to the side of the track. Now the rifleman faced Poo Koon, his weapon cocked and aimed at a point on the tusker's forehead midway between his eyes.

There was a tense twenty seconds of silence. Then Sing Noi said sullenly, "I will help. What do you want me to do?"

"There is a log to be lifted, that is all, and some packages to be taken from beneath the log," was the reply. "If you succeed, then you will get twenty ticals when we return. We are on our way to meet a merchant, and time is precious. Follow me . . . and if you try any tricks the boy will die."

He jerked his rifle toward Ba Thet, whose left arm had been twisted up his back. Over Ba Thet's head the other man was holding his long sword.

Poo Koon in Trouble

TEN MINUTES LATER POO KOON WAS EASING HIMSELF down the steep bank onto the sun-baked mud of the riverbed. Sing Noi showed no fear as he headed the big tusker upstream, but Ba Thet was afraid. It was like a nightmare.

Looking downstream, he could see several elephants with their *paijaiks* and *oozies* walking leisurely toward various piles of logs that were waiting for the river to rise. From the six-foot-wide stream flowing down the middle of the riverbed a flock of white birds rose, making the air chitter with their screaming cries, which sounded like, "You-did-it. You-did-it. You-did-it."

A giant hornbill flew overhead, its slow wingbeat making a faint *ssssh-sssss-ssssh* in the almost still air of the morning. It was the kind of day when everything should have been peaceful, yet Ba Thet's arm was twisted up his back, and the man with the sword kept jerking it up a little more, sending shivery thrills of pain through his shoulder. The one with the rifle walked by the side of Poo Koon, the muzzle of his weapon pointing at the tusker's head.

It was a beautiful morning, but for Ba Thet there was a threat of violent death in the air. He had heard about Mooser tribesmen. They were a lawless lot, and if anything went wrong they were capable of killing, then disappearing into the jungle.

Ba Thet's fears increased when they reached a place where a teak log had smashed down the rim of the riverbank. It had more than half buried itself in the rocks and debris it had brought down onto the riverbed, and six Mooser men were standing there, each one with a sword.

The man with the rifle looked up at Sing Noi and said, "There is a smashed cart under that log, and some packages. We know they are there, for we can see one. Order the elephant to lift the end of the log. There is a gap under it. The boy will crawl under and get the packages. There should be five."

Sing Noi frowned, shot a sideways glance at his nephew, then said, "Is it not better that one of you get the packages? My nephew is only a boy, and you can see that his arms are as thin as new bamboo shoots. He may not be strong enough."

He was interrupted with a curt "One of you will crawl under the log. I don't care which. We can be sure then that the elephant will not let the end of it

19

drop down. Now we are in a hurry. Get to work."

Sing Noi slid easily down the tusker's neck. Placing a hand on Ba Thet's shoulder, he whispered, "I shall get the packages, my nephew. I cannot let you take the risk. But be careful. I think these men are opium smugglers. They would not take such risks for . . . ooh!" Sing Noi lurched to one side, gasping, for the leader of the Moosers had darted over and jammed the muzzle of his rifle in his ribs.

"We are wasting time," the man snarled, threatening to strike Sing Noi again. "Hurry! I want one of you on the tusker and the other ready to get under the rocks when the log end is lifted. Waste any more time and I'll shoot you both, and the tusker."

"I will climb under the log," Sing Noi promised, and with a last imploring look at his nephew, he moved over to the pile of stones and debris.

Ba Thet was terrified. Only the fear that this Mooser man might shoot Poo Koon made him tell the tusker to kneel. He was trembling as he clambered onto the big neck and commanded Poo Koon to stand up. On other occasions when his uncle had allowed him to work the big tusker he had been thrilled and unafraid, for his uncle was always nearby to snap out a warning to Poo Koon if the tusker showed signs of doing the wrong thing.

Now he stared helplessly across to where his uncle was standing on the rocks. He wanted to plead to be allowed to crawl under the log himself and to ask his uncle to replace him on Poo Koon's neck, but the man with the rifle was already threatening him with the weapon.

Somehow Ba Thet managed to give the right word of command, and Poo Koon moved forward. From the age of about eighteen years the bull elephant had been working logs. Now he was twenty-five, fully grown, and thoroughly experienced in teak work. He seemed to understand well enough what was required, for he walked over, stood at the foot of the great pile of rubble, and stared at it as if making up his mind what to do. Ba Thet did not interfere, and after a minute Poo Koon quietly moved a small boulder out of the way. Then he placed his front feet as high up on the pile as he could and followed them with his hind feet.

The Mooser tribesmen watched in silence. Somewhere downriver an elephant gave a blasting roar of triumph. Ba Thet could guess what that meant. One of the other tuskers had just rolled a teak log off a pile, getting it nearer the middle of the channel for when the rains came and the river became a roaring torrent.

It was no use looking downstream, however. No help would come from that direction. Even if one of the other *oozies* looked up this way he would not see anything to make him take a second glance, for the Mooser men were all squatting down, keeping out of sight as much as possible.

Poo Koon climbed farther up the rubble until he was able to slip his tusks under the end of the teak log. A third of the log was buried under the stones, with rocks and masses of earth lying on the buried part.

Poo Koon had a length of about twelve feet to use as a lever. He took his time, shuffling his hind feet to make sure nothing slipped when he made his big effort. Finally, with his tusks hooked under the log and his trunk curled around the top, he began to heave. For a moment or so nothing happened, except that the thick neck muscles swelled until they were like the mooring lines of a big ship. Then came a slow creaking and crunching from the rocks.

The end of the log moved a little—up—up—up!—inch by inch—while Poo Koon grunted and snorted under the strain. Ba Thet looked down to where his uncle was crouched close by the gap where the log went under the rocks. There was an opening there, and it was widening little by little.

Suddenly the leader of the Mooser tribesmen yelled, "In! Go in! Get in! There is room. Quick!" Hurrying across, he jabbed the muzzle of his gun into Sing Noi's ribs.

Sing Noi had been looking anxiously into the opening. Now he turned with a hint of despair in his eyes and said, "The packages have slipped farther in. I can't reach them."

"Then crawl in!" the Mooser leader roared, and jabbed him again with the gun muzzle.

22

For a moment the gaze of Sing Noi and his nephew met. Ba Thet could read the agonized plea in his uncle's eyes. He was asking Ba Thet to make sure Poo Koon did not let the end of the log slip down. Then, urged on by the prodding gun muzzle, he crawled into the opening. For a moment or so his legs were visible as he wriggled through the narrow gap between the rocks; then they were through and lost to sight.

Ba Thet shouted to his uncle to hurry, for Poo Koon was already showing signs of tiring. He was making a tremendous effort, and must have a rest. Not even his great strength was enough to keep the log end up. He began to ease his upward thrust.

There was an ominous crunching and grinding from the rocks as the ones that had been lifted settled down again. Ba Thet shrieked in horror, sure that his uncle must have been crushed under the rocks, and he tried to get the tusker to heave at the log again.

Poo Koon was breathing heavily. He was too wise to make another attempt immediately. Then the leader of the Moosers yelled angrily, "Quiet . . . he's all right. If you listen, you'll hear him."

His heart thumping, Ba Thet listened. Sure enough he could hear his uncle talking. Sing Noi's voice was muffled, but he was telling the leader of the Moosers that he was in a small cave, and that when the gap was opened up once more he would be able to hand out the packages. They were all there, five of them, lying in the mashed wreckage of a village cart.

Ba Thet blew out a great sigh of relief, then stretched his right foot so that he could tickle Poo Koon behind the ear to show that his efforts had been appreciated. The big tusker curled back his trunk until the tip was within touching distance. Ba Thet grabbed it and squeezed it for a moment, at which mark of approval Poo Koon burbled his delight.

There was no more time for rejoicing, however, for the Mooser leader was demanding further efforts. He ordered Ba Thet to make the tusker lift the end of the teak log again.

When Ba Thet called on Poo Koon for another heave, the contented burblings stopped. For a moment or so there was silence; then the long trunk went up and the tusks slid under the log. With the muscles cording on neck and back legs, the big tusker heaved again.

Once more, as the end of the log rose, there was a warning crunching and grumbling from the rocks in the pile as if they did not like being disturbed. A thin arm appeared from the black gap under the log, and in Sing Noi's hand was a package of opium.

The Mooser leader snatched it away and tossed it to one of his men. He started to say something to the unseen Sing Noi when there was a sudden grinding of rock on rock. All eyes turned at the sound, and there were yells of alarm as a boulder on top of the pile swayed uneasily.

The boulder moved and rolled to one side, adding

more weight to Poo Koon's burden. The strain proved too much for him, and the big tusker gave a muffled squeal of protest. The log slipped downward a little, and brought still more crunching and grinding from the rocks.

Ba Thet screamed for his elephant to make another effort. "Heave . . . heave . . . *heave!*"

Poo Koon responded at once. His neck muscles tightened as he lunged upward with all his great strength, and as he did there was a ringing crack. It sounded to Ba Thet as if someone had snapped a thick piece of living bamboo. A moment later the tusker staggered, and Ba Thet almost lost his seat. In the same instant something cream-colored, nearly two feet long, and thicker than a man's arm clattered down the rocks.

Ba Thet stared at it, unable to believe what he saw. The thing now lying wedged between two small rocks was part of an elephant's tusk! He looked in amazement at Poo Koon's head, but before he could make up his mind that what he feared was true, Poo Koon uncurled his trunk from the teak log and, lifting it high, made the air tingle with a scream of such wildness that even the Mooser men cringed. Ba Thet clapped his hands to his ears. He had heard many elephants trumpet; he had heard them scream in anger and in rage; but he had never before heard a scream like this one.

He realized within seconds what had happened.

Poo Koon's left tusk had snapped off. He would not be the first elephant with only one tusk—some were born that way, and still worked teak as well as the next elephant. But the break had exposed the big nerve in the tusk, and the scream that had sent feeding birds wheeling into the air had been dragged out of Poo Koon by the sudden, excruciating pain. He was getting a mammoth-sized toothache. The exposed nerve was sending wave after wave of pain through his jaw—enough to drive any animal mad.

Poo Koon swung around, stumbled off the pile of debris and stormed across the mud toward the stream in the riverbed, while Ba Thet clung like a limpet to his seat, himself petrified with fear. He could only hope that the tusker would not remember he carried a rider. If he did, then the chances were he would swing his trunk over his head, pluck Ba Thet from his seat, and dash him to the ground. Pain-maddened elephants had done that often enough, as Ba Thet knew.

Of course, Poo Koon could not know what was hurting him, but he seemed to want to get his broken tusk into the water, to feel what should be its soothing coolness damping down the frightening shock waves of agony shooting through his head.

When he reached the stream coursing down the wide bed of the river, he dipped in the end of his trunk and sucked up gallons and gallons of water. Then he curled up his trunk and blew a jet of the river water onto his broken tusk—and onto the exposed nerve!

The river water was not really cold, but it was much cooler than the nerve and the effect was disastrous. It must have felt as if a red-hot dagger had been thrust deep into Poo Koon's tusk. The shattering intensity of the pain made even his thick, columnlike legs quiver. For a second or so he seemed to be on the point of collapse. Then he screamed and began to run downriver.

Ba Thet could have dismounted while Poo Koon was sucking up water, but he had stayed on the tusker's neck in the hope that after a few minutes he might be able to soothe his elephant and perhaps guide him back to camp.

That hope was shattered within a minute. Farther downstream, where a number of *oozies* were busily piling logs closer to the middle of the riverbed, two men heard Poo Koon's first wild scream. Realizing that something out of the ordinary must have happened, they turned their tuskers upstream, urging them to a shuffling trot in an effort to discover what had gone wrong and to see if they could help.

They saw Poo Koon reach the river, draw up water, then squirt it on his tusk. There seemed to be nothing out of the ordinary about that, but seconds later the big tusker screamed again. Then he thundered toward them, his great feet making a hollow drumming on the dried mud, his trunk curled up and the tip in his mouth. There was no mistaking what that meant. For some reason Poo Koon was coming at them to fight.

Ba Thet managed to scream a warning. "Get away! He's gone mad!" The warning was scarcely needed. The *oozies* and their elephants knew the signs only too well—the angry screaming, the tightly coiled trunk, both told the same story of a fighting-mad tusker.

The other tuskers started to turn, but two turned toward each other and lost valuable seconds. One of them managed to get around and begin to run, but the other was put off his stride by the momentary collision. In those few seconds his *oozie*, a man of long experience, seemed to realize that if they did begin to run, Poo Koon would catch them. Even the most agile of elephants needs a few seconds to get into a full run, and Poo Koon was already coming at top speed.

The *oozie* did what he probably considered was the wisest thing. He turned his mount to face Poo Koon. More elephants are killed by being stabbed in the rear by the tusks of an attacker than by a head-on collision, and his own tusker was a huge beast. He was older than Poo Koon and had fought before.

After swinging his tusker around to meet Poo Koon, the *oozie* slithered adroitly down the great shoulders and ran for his life. To stay on his mount would not help. The battle had to be one of elephant versus elephant, and no unarmed human being could help one way or the other.

Ba Thet closed his eyes as he saw the other *oozie* make his getaway; it was something he would have liked to do. But Poo Koon was tearing along at at least twenty miles an hour. Only a fool would fling himself to the ground from a height of nine feet, and the sunbaked mud was iron hard.

Eyes wide with terror, he saw the other tusker curl his big trunk and hunch his massive shoulders to take the shock of the collision. He lowered his head a little to offer the broad front of his forehead to Poo Koon, and a second or so later the two big bulls met.

Crunch!

With his forehead a big elephant can push over a mighty tree. The forehead bones are thick enough to withstand tremendous battering shocks, and the impact of this collision, which would have dropped any other animal senseless, merely rocked the two bulls backward.

Ba Thet had tried to prepare for the collision, bracing himself by gripping Poo Koon's thick neck as best he could with his legs, and grabbing at the soft loose skin behind the tusker's head, but it did not help him in the least. Poo Koon had been traveling at the speed of a champion hundred-yards sprinter. When he hit the other bull he was stopped dead in his tracks. There was nothing to hold Ba Thet on. His hands tore free from their grip and he sailed over Poo

Koon's head in a forward dive that landed him squarely on the other tusker's forehead.

Despite their thick bony foreheads both tuskers were momentarily dazed. They reeled backward and shook their heads.

Ba Thet clawed frantically for a grip that would keep him from falling. But as the elephant shook his head he rolled sideways onto a tusk and from there to the ground, his hand sliding across the tusker's right eye.

Ba Thet's left foot hit the ground; he reeled sideways, then went down with a jolt that drove the air from his lungs and sent blinding flashes of light through his head. He rolled onto his back, spread-eagled, unable to move or think.

A yard or so away Poo Koon was already recovering. With his tusk still sending vicious stabs of pain through his jaw and head, he lunged forward again, screaming, with Ba Thet almost in the path of his big feet.

Poo Koon Must Die!

ONE CHANCE IN A MILLION SAVED BA THET FROM DEATH in the short time he lay on the ground, shaken and not quite knowing where he was. When he scraped his hand across the other bull elephant's eye, the animal's vision was blurred momentarily. Unable to see Poo Koon, the tusker turned to the right. Poo Koon was already lunging in again, and had to swerve in order to get at his enemy.

That swerve saved Ba Thet, for Poo Koon's right forefoot thumped down on the mud only inches away from his right thigh. Had his body come under the crushing weight, he would have died. As it was, he instinctively rolled over and, still gasping for breath, managed to get to his knees.

He was in time to see Poo Koon get in a glancing blow with his undamaged tusk at the other bull's shoulder, drawing blood and bringing a scream of mingled rage and pain. Wheeling around, the injured bull charged in.

After one terrified glance at the mighty battlers, Ba Thet staggered away, making for the stream in the dried-up riverbed. He was dazed and shaking, and he almost fell into the water. He remained on hands and knees for half a minute, while the coolness began to revive him. Then he lowered his head and sucked up a mouthful of the water.

Sixty yards away the two bulls were hammering

away at each other, charging again and again. Poo Koon was big, but the other, older bull had the advantage of experience. He had fought a number of times. Poo Koon was mad, but the other bull had fear to help him. He knew that a false move might mean a death-dealing thrust from Poo Koon's remaining tusk.

A chance blow finally ended the fight. The older bull's coiled trunk caught the end of Poo Koon's broken tusk. The effect was to multiply the agony, and for seconds Poo Koon could only stand and tremble, his legs almost giving way at the dagger thrusts of pain. Had the older bull charged then he could have gained a quick victory, but he was glad enough of the chance to break off the fight. With a defiant squeal he turned and scuttled away as fast as his legs could carry him.

Ba Thet hurried upstream when he saw his tusker coming slowly toward the river. He watched Poo Koon dip his trunk into the stream and suck up water. For a moment the trunk coiled around as if the big tusker again meant to squirt water on the aching tusk. Then he must have remembered that the last time he did that the pain had been even greater, so instead, he swung his trunk up and squirted a dozen gallons of water over his back. After that he turned and walked slowly toward the riverbank and the track leading back to the teak camp.

33

Once he was sure Poo Koon was really about to leave the riverbed, Ba Thet sank to his knees. He sagged forward, the weight of his body on his arms, his head drooping.

In the short space of an hour or less his whole happy world had crashed to ruin about him. In a few days he and his uncle were to have collected their pay for a season's teak hauling. They could have gone back to their village and, with their earnings, finally paid off the debt they owed on their elephant. Now Sing Noi was a prisoner under the pile of rocks and rubble and Poo Koon had gone mad.

And he *was* mad! The pain of the broken tusk had driven him crazy. Ba Thet groaned at the thought. Nor was this the madness of musth, a fever that gripped most bull elephants once a year, but which

passed off after a week or two. Poo Koon's madness was different. He was really mad.

Then Ba Thet's body stiffened as a terrible thought occurred to him. Poo Koon had headed back to camp! If he met any of the men—the cook, an *oozie*, a *paijaik*, or Bill Johnson—it could be disastrous. In his present terrible rage Poo Koon might attack anyone.

The thought that he could meet Mr. Johnson brought another fear. Mr. Johnson might shoot Poo Koon.

That made Ba Thet forget his weariness. Fear for the tusker drove everything else out of his mind. He began to run.

If he could get to the camp before Poo Koon he would beg some rice and salt from the cook. With this he might be able to coax the big tusker into a better frame of mind. Surely the pain of a broken tusk could not last very long. Ba Thet had once seen Mr. Johnson saw a few inches off the end of another bull's tusks when they were getting too long and too sharp. Of course, Bill Johnson was always careful not to get anywhere near the nerve end.

But now the first thing Ba Thet had to do was to warn everyone that Poo Koon was on the rampage. He must also tell Bill Johnson about Sing Noi's predicament.

The moment he thought of that, some of Ba Thet's worries for his uncle abated. Bill Johnson could do almost anything. Ba Thet had seen men brought into

35

camp suffering from terrible injuries, but Johnson had doctored them and they had survived. Village women sometimes came in, seeking medical help either for themselves or their children, and they never went away without being given some help. Surely Sing Noi could be rescued.

The farther he went down the dried-up riverbed, the more evidence there was that news of Poo Koon had already gone before him. Not a single elephant was at work stacking logs. No man could be seen anywhere. They had all fled, taking their elephants with them. They knew that a maddened tusker could wreak havoc, sometimes killing or maiming men and animals before someone managed to shoot him. That was what usually happened when a tusker went mad. He had to die.

"Not Poo Koon," Ba Thet groaned as he plodded on. "He is *our* elephant. If he dies we are beggars."

As he trotted on he was straining his ears to catch some sound that would tell him what was happening. A shout from an *oozie* would have been music to his ears, but he seemed to be the only living person in the area. Birds flew overhead and a magnificent sambar stag cautiously came out from a clump of bushes and stared across the riverbed. He had been waiting to drink and now that the men and elephants had gone, he was about to risk a trot across to the water. He drew back at the sight of Ba Thet, but came out again when the boy had passed.

Breathless, Ba Thet finally turned away from the river and climbed the bank where it was trodden down to an easy slope. This was where the elephants came down to pile logs on the riverbed. The camp was about four hundred yards away.

No one could mistake the track for anything but one made by elephants. It was as if every one of them had the same length of stride, for the track was pitted with round holes where the big feet trod and re-trod as they made their way to and from the camp. When the rainy season came the holes would be muddy pools.

Ba Thet was not thinking about that sort of thing now. His ears were strained to catch the first sounds from the camp. As he trotted near and the silence continued, his fears increased. The sudden *ooo-ooo-ooo-ooo* of a family of monkeys moving through the treetops to his right made his heart leap in fear until he recognized the sound.

Getting to the top of a little hill, he saw a thin column of smoke rising into the sunshine. It was the camp, and the smoke from the kitchen helped kill the worst of his fears. If Chaung Thak was cooking, then Poo Koon could not have been here. His optimism died a minute later when he reached the clearing in which their camp stood. The thin pillar of smoke was not rising from the cook's fire, but from the dying ashes of what had been the cook's shelter.

As for the camp itself—Ba Thet stood and stared

in disbelief. If a giant bulldozer had been driven backward and forward through the camp, and the driver had been determined to level everything to the ground, the devastation could not have been worse. Every building was down. True, they had been flimsily built of bamboo and atap leaves, but now they were heaps of smashed bamboo and atap. The rampaging Poo Koon had destroyed everything. A patch of green to one side had been Bill Johnson's tent. Now it was a ruffled heap of canvas, with odd little bulges showing through the green where a camp bed, a box, and other items had refused to be flattened completely.

His throat dry, his heart thumping, Ba Thet stood and stared—and waited. He was waiting for someone to come, for someone to speak, for a movement to say there was some life in the camp. But the only thing moving was that slender pale-blue column of smoke rising from the ashes of the cook's shelter.

They had all gone, even Bill Johnson. Poo Koon had driven them away.

Then, in those first frightening moments, fear of the big tusker was blotted out by an even worse fear—fear for his uncle. If they had all gone, who would help him to free Sing Noi? To get him out from under the teak log and the rocks would take a score of men *and* elephants, and now there was no one but himself.

Filled with this new terror, he called, "Hallo . . .

hallo . . . hallo!" and jumped nervously when he got an answer almost at once.

From a tree outside the camp area came an anxious question, "Has he gone? Where is he?"

"Chaung Thak!" Ba Thet could have wept with joy at hearing a human voice, and he turned and ran toward the unseen speaker. "Where are you? Are you hurt? Was it Poo Koon? Where are you?"

Chaung Thak, the teak wallah's cook, slid down a tree and came limping forward. He was an oldish man. Once he had been acknowledged as the finest *oozie* ever to sit astride an elephant, and had been paid to ride "fierce" tuskers, but one day he had taken one chance too many. A blow from a trunk had permanently damaged a leg and his days as an *oozie* were ended. Now he walked with a limp, and cooked.

"You ask if I am all right?" His voice was a sarcastic shriek as he dusted his shirt and pulled prickles from his hands. "That devil of an elephant would have skinned me and eaten me alive if he could have got at me. He was so near getting me that I even forgot my limp." As he said that the anger faded from his face and a twinkle came into his eyes. With a chuckle he added, "Fear is a wonderful thing, Ba Thet. It can make even an old man feel young. No man ever ran so quick as I, or climbed a tree at such speed."

He felt in his shorts' pocket and brought out a

little pipe. Slowly he stuffed the bowl with tobacco, then going over to the burned wreck of his cooking shelter, pushed a splinter of bamboo into the fire and lit the pipe.

Gently rubbing his elbows and knees, where climbing the tree had grazed the skin, he called to Ba Thet, who was poking among the ruins of what had been the shelter used by him and his uncle Sing Noi.

"What a devil Poo Koon is. He always did things better than any other tusker, and no other tusker could have flattened a camp as this camp is flattened. What went wrong? Is he musth?"

"No, no, not musth," Ba Thet protested, and poured out his story of the smugglers and of how Poo Koon's tusk had been broken off.

Chaung Thak's eyes went round as rice balls. "Mooser men," he murmured, blowing a thin column of smoke upward. "And carrying opium. That is a strange tale, Ba Thet. I know they grow the poppy, and I know they smuggle their opium, but they have never been on our side of the Keng Oom Valley before. And you say one of them has a rifle?"

Ba Thet nodded, then asked anxiously, "What can we do for my uncle? He is like a fighting cock in a cage, except that there is no door to this cage. He cannot get out unless we have elephants to lift the log and the rocks. Where is everyone? There were no elephants, no *oozies,* not even a *paijaik* on the river-bed."

40

"Where would you be if a devil like Poo Koon came rampaging along?" the old man asked soberly. "I expect the *oozies* have taken their elephants out of Poo Koon's way, and the *paijaiks* will have gone with them."

"But where is Mr. Johnson?" Ba Thet demanded. "He must be told."

"He went off to look for some green pigeons for the pot," Chaung Thak said, and added, "but I wouldn't be too anxious to have him back if I were you. What do you think he will say when he sees what your tusker has done?"

Ba Thet had no answer for that. There was a cold shivery feeling inside him.

"What about my uncle?" he asked, after a short pause.

"Wait until Bill Johnson returns," Chaung Thak advised. "He will—oh! oh! Maybe this is he. Yes. He is coming."

Chaung Thak might be getting old, but there was nothing wrong with his ears and he had caught the sound of someone approaching. A minute later Bill Johnson came into the clearing and stood staring at the scene of devastation. He had half a dozen green pigeons slung at his belt, and he handed them to Chaung Thak, then listened in silence to Ba Thet's apologetic story.

"I'll have a mug of tea," the teak wallah told Chaung Thak. Then he said to Ba Thet, "Don't worry

too much about this. I have had camps wrecked before—but then it was by an elephant on musth. You
are sure Poo Koon hasn't gone musth?"

"He was all right until his tusk was broken," Ba

Thet faltered. "No sign of musth. My uncle, Sing Noi, would have seen it surely."

"Yes, of course," Johnson agreed. Then he said more briskly, "Chaung Thak, forget the tea. Go and find the *oozies*. If we are to rescue Sing Noi we'll need four of the largest of the tuskers. Er . . . let me see. Yes, bring Kyauk Seine, San Shwe O, and Kya Sine. If you can find another to match them, he'll make up the four."

"I could be clearing up the kitchen and making you some tea if Ba Thet went for the tuskers," the old man suggested. "He is younger than I, and has no limp."

"Did men make excuses when the tusker broke your leg?" Johnson asked. With a grin he added, "Go on, rogue. As cook you lead too easy a life . . . and I've seen your limp vanish when you thought no one was looking. I want the boy here with me."

"Yes, sir," Chaung Thak agreed. "I just thought that any fool can find elephants, but it takes a man with skill to make tea the way you like it."

"Out!" Johnson ordered, but there was a twitch to his lips. His cook *was* an old rogue, but Johnson could not help liking him. Chaung Thak shrugged and hobbled slowly away. Johnson watched him for a moment. Then, turning to Ba Thet, he said with a smile, "Blow the fire to life, Ba Thet, and stop worrying about your uncle. In an hour we'll have him back in camp. I'll have a cup of tea and then get my rifle."

"Rifle, sir?" Ba Thet asked, beginning to blow on the fire.

"Have you ever had a toothache?" Johnson asked. When Ba Thet shook his head, Johnson went on. "It is the kind of pain that can keep a man awake at night no matter how tired he is—and a man's teeth are small."

"That is true," Ba Thet agreed, but he was puzzled.

"When a bull elephant like Poo Koon gets a toothache," Johnson said, and now his voice was grimmer, "you can look out for trouble. You can see what he has done here. Suppose he came around when we were trying to dig out your uncle. What could we do? Run, and leave your uncle under the rocks? Your uncle has got to be rescued quickly, before the monsoon breaks and fills the riverbed with water. So—I shall take my rifle. I hope I won't have to use it, but a man's life is more valuable than an elephant. Do you agree?"

"Yes, sir," said Ba Thet, but his heart was sick with worry. He knew Johnson was right. The pain-maddened elephant could stop the rescue work if he came back. Ba Thet closed his eyes and hoped Poo Koon would stay away.

He blew the fire to a white heat, which quickly boiled a kettle of water. Johnson saw the misery in the boy's eyes and gave him a cup of strong, sweet tea. They were sitting down to drink when the tuskers arrived.

Johnson wasted no time. He told the *oozies* what they were to do, and why Poo Koon was temporarily mad. When the elephants were ready they were to go up the river with dragging chains, ropes, axes, picks, and shovels, and free Sing Noi.

While the *oozies* and their *paijaiks* were collecting the equipment, Johnson called Ba Thet and Chaung Thak to clear the tent canvas and stack the equipment lying under it. The camp bed had been broken and the canvas bath would never stand on its own legs again, but the case with the high-velocity rifle seemed to have escaped injury.

Johnson examined the rifle carefully, checking it to make sure Poo Koon had not actually put a big foot on it and damaged the mechanism. When a man faced an angry elephant a misfire could bring sudden, awful death.

Ba Thet stood to one side and watched as Johnson made sure that all was correct with the rifle. He watched him slip a cartridge into the breech, look along the sights, then eject the cartridge. Noticing him, Johnson said, "I don't want to use it, Ba Thet. I don't shoot elephants because I like it, only if I am forced to."

"Yes, sir." Ba Thet turned away. He had a feeling Johnson would have to shoot. Why he felt that way he did not know, but he was afraid.

He knew Johnson was worried, not only at the thought that Poo Koon might appear on the scene when they were digging Sing Noi out, but also by the weather. In the past hour the sunshine had dimmed a little. There was a vague haziness in the sky—and the heaviness that comes before a thunderstorm.

Men and boys all knew the signs, and at any other time they would have been delighted. The season's logs were stacked on the riverbed. All they were waiting for now was the rain, and the floods that would come pouring down from the hills, floods that would lift the heavy balks of teak off the mud and float them downstream in a rushing, swirling mass to the broad river miles away. From there they would eventually be carried to the sawmills at Bangkok.

Now no one wanted the rain until Sing Noi had been rescued. If the river flooded while he was held prisoner among the rocks, he could drown. Therefore, when Johnson gave the word to march, there was no hesitation at all. Every man and boy was eager to get the job done. Once Sing Noi was free, they would welcome the hissing thunder of monsoon rain.

Slinging his rifle over his shoulder, Bill Johnson handed his shotgun to Chaung Thak. The only uneasiness was among the elephants. They knew that one of their number had been wounded by another elephant.

The most eager person of all was Ba Thet. He was confident that once his uncle was free, he would be

able to soothe Poo Koon. He had been a close friend
of the big tusker for years, for the bull had grown up
in their village, and Ba Thet had never before known
him to run amok.

Johnson looked tight-lipped as he strode along
ahead of the others, his rifle ready, with the safety
catch in the "off" position. Where Poo Koon was

now no one knew, but they might see him before the day was out.

Slowing down, Johnson called Ba Thet. "Have you ever dealt with Poo Koon when he was angry or hurt?" he asked.

Ba Thet shook his head slowly as he tried to remember any such occasion. "I have never seen Poo Koon angry until this morning. He is the best teak elephant in—"

"Yes, yes, I know," Johnson interrupted. "I'm worried in case he appears when we are getting your uncle free. If he should come, do you think he would listen to you?"

Ba Thet's heart gave a tremendous flip-flop as he remembered how angry Poo Koon had been immediately after his tusk was snapped off.

Realizing the boy was nervous, Johnson said, "All right, don't worry. I'll handle him if he comes."

"Mr. Johnson," Ba Thet said hesitantly, "you will not shoot him?"

"I don't want to shoot him," Johnson replied. "He is a good teak elephant and I know that Sing Noi and your father still owe money on him. On the other hand, we cannot allow him to interfere when we are rescuing Sing Noi. You agree?"

"Yes, sir." Ba Thet sounded unhappy.

"If he does come," Johnson said, "are you prepared to go out and try to lead him away? It is either that or shooting him. We'll have the working elephants here, and their *oozies*. You know what could happen if a pain-crazed tusker as big and strong as Poo Koon got among them? If he comes it means either you go out and lead him away, or I'll have to kill him."

Ba Thet had to swallow a choking lump in his throat before he could answer. In a shaky voice he said, "I will go out and lead him away. I am sure he will obey me."

"I hope he will," Johnson said, "but if he won't, then you'll have to dodge out of the way and leave him to me." He patted the stock of his rifle and Ba Thet nodded glumly. He had once seen Bill Johnson shoot a gaur, a bisonlike animal weighing about a ton. The gaur had dropped kicking at the first shot.

A few minutes later they came to the place where the bank had been carefully broken to make a slope where the elephants could get to the riverbed. They went down one by one. Overhead the sky had already changed drastically. There was a grayness over the world, and even the birds were quiet. It seemed as if everything was waiting for the first roar of thunder from the hills. When the rain did come, the mud on which they were now marching would be covered with a foaming torrent, its depth increasing hourly as waters from the hills in the north drained into the rivulets that fed the main stream.

No time was wasted when they got to the rocks, where there was now no sign of the smugglers. Ba Thet was sent to tell his uncle that rescuers were here, and to pass through to him a length of hollow bamboo that had been filled with water. That had been Chaung Thak's idea. With the water went a packet of hastily prepared rice cakes.

"All will soon be well, Uncle," Ba Thet said, as he struggled to pass the precious two feet of bamboo through the narrow gap between log and rocks. "Mr. Johnson is here with four of the big tuskers and most of the men from the camp."

"It makes my heart glad," Sing Noi called out, gratefully taking in the bamboo water holder. "It has not been pleasant to crouch here alone. You have done well. Is Poo Koon here? I heard him scream as if he had been hurt. After that the Mooser men came, threatening me. They said you had gone off with the elephant."

Ba Thet told his uncle about the breaking of Poo Koon's tusk and about his maniacal rage afterward. He did not mention the devastated camp, not wanting to add to his uncle's anxiety.

"And where is he now?" Sing Noi persisted.

"I think he is sulking somewhere near the camp," Ba Thet said, and was glad his uncle seemed satisfied. He stayed while Sing Noi drank the water and ate the rice cakes. Then Bill Johnson called him away. The elephants were ready.

"I shall rejoice with you in a few minutes, my uncle," Ba Thet said, wriggling his arm through the gap so that he could hold Sing Noi's hand for a moment. "All will be well very soon." He gave his uncle's hand a reassuring squeeze, then left him to go and watch the first attempt to drag the largest boulder off the pile. Bill Johnson said that if this heavy mass of rock was moved, one of the tuskers would be able to lift the end of the log, as Poo Koon had lifted it, and so allow Sing Noi to be dragged through the widened gap below.

The four elephants were lined up and the *oozies* were watching their *paijaiks* link the hawsers to the dragging chains, when there came a warning shout from a man posted on the riverbank above.

"Mr. Johnson! He is coming! I can see Poo Koon!" He pointed to a small outjutting tongue of land where the river narrowed. Every head turned and no one spoke as they watched and waited to see if Poo Koon would appear.

"Finish linking the elephants," Johnson ordered, and as the *paijaiks* turned to obey, he called to Ba Thet. "Do you want to go out to Poo Koon if he does show up? It will be dangerous, but he might recognize you and come to his senses. If he obeyed you it would save a lot of trouble, and I wouldn't have to shoot him. I don't want to do that. If you are prepared to go out and try to soothe him, I'll be just behind you. If he doesn't listen to you I'll be ready. You need only get out of the way and I'll be there to shoot him."

"Yes, sir," said Ba Thet, but he felt heartsick.

"He's here!" Suddenly half a dozen voices began to shout that Poo Koon had just come around the little headland.

"Well, what about it? Are you going?" Johnson asked. "I don't want him to get too near these tuskers. They're nervous of him already."

"I go." Ba Thet's voice rose little above a whisper. He loved Poo Koon, and if the big tusker had to be shot, his family would lose years and years of hard saving.

Ba Thet began to walk out toward Poo Koon, who was staring silently at the men and elephants gathered near where Sing Noi was trapped. As Ba Thet hurried toward him, the tusker raised his trunk and made the air quiver with a shrill trumpet blast of rage. He tucked his trunk tip into his mouth and, at the queer shuffling trot characteristic of elephants, headed for the boy.

Ba Thet began calling at once. "*Hmit! Hmit!* Do you hear me? *Hmit!*" His order for the elephant to kneel was wasted, for Poo Koon showed no sign of slackening his speed.

Bill Johnson roared a command. "Stand clear, Ba Thet. Stand clear. I'll fire in front of him; that may stop him."

Ba Thet ran a dozen yards to one side, then turned to see what would happen. He heard the heavy rifle crack, and an echo come from the far side of the valley. Poo Koon slowed for a moment, screamed defiantly, and came on again at his quickest trot.

Bill Johnson dropped to one knee and took careful aim. His first shot had been deliberately aimed wide. Now he must shoot to kill.

A Shot from the Jungle

AIMING FOR THAT WEAK SPOT IN THE FRONT OF THE head where a bullet can get through to the brain, Bill Johnson took first pressure on the rifle trigger. As he did so, there was a crack from the other bank, and a thin puff of smoke was seen in the bushes. Almost immediately the teak wallah fell over backward, his rifle firing into the air as it sprang out of his grasp.

The two shots sounded so close together that anyone could have been forgiven for thinking one sound was merely the echo of the first. But Ba Thet knew better. He had been looking at Poo Koon, and past the tusker to the far bank. He had seen the wisp of blue-gray smoke and, a moment later, a hurried movement as men drew back from the bushes.

Shocked though he was, he realized what had happened. The Mooser men had not wanted to leave their smuggled opium behind. They had crossed the

54

river and had been hiding in a place where they could see what happened to the rescue attempt. When Mr. Johnson fired his first shot in an attempt to scare Poo Koon away, they had imagined he had seen them and was shooting at them, so one of them had fired back. And now Mr. Johnson lay sprawled on the mud.

Ba Thet could only stand and stare in horror. He saw the Mooser men vanish into the jungle, then half turned at the commotion behind him. There was pandemonium among the *oozies* and *paijaiks* at what had happened. But that was followed by sudden panic as Poo Koon, after being startled into coming to a full stop by the shots, began to recover. With a scream of defiance he shuffled forward again.

The *paijaiks* did not hesitate, but ran for the river-bank and hastily scrambled to the top where they would be safe. The *oozies* quickly turned their elephants around so they could shed their dragging harness by allowing it to slide free over their necks and heads. No one willingly faced a mad elephant.

Chaung Thak was the only one who did not move. He stood and stared, as if he could not believe that Mr. Johnson was lying out there, with a pain-crazed elephant shuffling in his direction.

Ba Thet was terrified, but he ran past the limp figure of the teak wallah toward Poo Koon. As he ran he yelled, *"Hmit! Hmit!* Listen to me, you old fool. *Hmit!"* The phrase "old fool" was one he often used as a term of endearment when he was washing the tusker. It must have penetrated the red mist of hate and pain in Poo Koon's tormented brain, for he slowed down.

He was ten yards from Bill Johnson, six yards from the boy. His trunk tip came out of his mouth and swung out toward Ba Thet.

"What's the matter with you?" Ba Thet was trembling. If Poo Koon lunged forward now, swinging his heavy trunk, only a wild leap would avoid a tragedy. The big tusker's eyes were bloodshot, and his shattered tusk added to his frightening appearance, yet Ba Thet dared not retreat.

"We'll make it right," Ba Thet said soothingly. "You stop behaving like a silly old fool. Now *hmit!* Do you hear me? *Hmit!*"

For perhaps ten seconds boy and elephant faced one another, and the battle hung in the balance. The familiar voice and figure had somehow brought a moment of sanity. Poo Koon remembered Ba Thet.

Then from behind the boy Bill Johnson groaned and began trying to roll over onto his side. That broke the spell. Poo Koon's eyes took on their wild glare again. He lifted his trunk and squealed, then came on once more. If Ba Thet had obeyed his first, frightened impulse, which was to run, Bill Johnson would have died in the next twenty seconds, for the tusker's eyes were fixed on him.

"Run!" An *oozie*, riding his elephant away from

danger but looking back at the drama on the river mud, screamed a warning. "Run . . . *run!*"

Ba Thet stood his ground. Four yards behind him Bill Johnson was trying to turn off his back onto his side, one arm flailing the air weakly. Poo Koon had never seemed so big to Ba Thet. His trunk swung up for a blow that would smash the boy out of the way.

Crack . . . crack! The twin roars came from Bill Johnson's double-barreled shotgun, and the man who squeezed the triggers was Chaung Thak. While the *oozies* and *paijaiks* were scattering in panic, the old man raised the weapon at the crucial moment and fired both barrels almost simultaneously.

The double report stopped Poo Koon dead, his big feet sliding on the mud and throwing up little spurts of dark-brown dust. Ba Thet looked up for a moment into his elephant's eyes, then grabbed Bill Johnson by the shoulders and began to drag him aside. If Poo Koon had lunged forward he could have got two victims in as many seconds, but the two thunder bangs from the shotgun turned him about. He could panic as quickly as anyone, and seconds later the mud was shaking under the thump of his big feet as he scuttled away as quickly as he had come.

There were yells of triumph from the boys who had scrambled up the bank, but no sound came from either Ba Thet or Chaung Thak. The old man was ruefully rubbing his right shoulder. He had never fired a heavy shotgun, and in his hurry had not pressed the butt into his shoulder. As a result the kickback of the gun had given him a blow that he would feel for some time to come.

The moment Ba Thet realized the danger was over he stopped dragging the white man. Now that the crisis was over he began to tremble, and after a moment or so was forced to sink down to his knees and lower his head. The riverbed and the hills on either side seemed to be swirling around and around.

At a yell from Chaung Thak the watching *paijaiks* scrambled down the bank and carried Bill Johnson off the mud, then looked to the old man for further orders. Chaung Thak was too proud to let the *paijaiks* think he could not handle a gun. He stopped rubbing his bruised shoulder. There was a grin of triumph and pride on his face as he waved and said, "Make a carrier from bamboo. We must get him back to camp. One of you fetch his rifle. As for them"— and he pointed downriver to where the tuskers and the *oozies* were now scrambling up the bank onto the jungle track—"what *men* they are, eh?" And he spat.

As the *paijaiks* hurried to collect bamboo to make a rough-and-ready stretcher, Chaung Thak walked slowly over to where Ba Thet still knelt on the mud. He placed a hand on the boy's head, ruffled his sweat-damp hair for a moment, then said, "I would not have expected a son of my own to have shown more courage, Ba Thet. You are not a boy—you are a man!"

While the *paijaiks* split bamboos and wove them into a stretcher, Chaung Thak went over to the rocks to tell Sing Noi that there had been an interruption, but that they would be back soon to rescue him. In an hour, he promised, and then turned and walked away, leaving Sing Noi pleading for someone to stay and keep him company.

Back at the camp, with the green tent once more erected, Bill Johnson was laid on blankets, while *oozies* and *paijaiks* stood in little groups, murmuring uneasily, and wondering what would happen now.

When Chaung Thak came out of the tent there was a hush.

"He is not dead—yet," the old man announced, and added, "Who brought back the big rifle? Ah, give it to me." He took the heavy weapon and examined it while men and boys watched in respectful silence.

Ba Thet could see an ugly gash in the woodwork of the gun butt. It looked as if a sharp-pointed pick had been driven into it. The dark-brown wood, lovingly polished over the years, was badly scarred. Something had struck it a terrific blow, but for the moment old Chaung Thak could not think what. Ba Thet gave him a clue when he asked, "Did anyone hear a second shot from the far side of the river? The Mooser men were hiding there. One of them had a gun. I think he fired at Mr. Johnson. The bullet hit the rifle and damaged it as you see."

"But what made the teak wallah fall?" one of the

oozies asked anxiously. "Did the bullet go in his head. His face was swollen, and his forehead."

Chaung Thak shook his head. "The bullet hit the rifle, and the force of the blow knocked the metal-work against Mr. Johnson's forehead. I think that is what happened."

He stroked his chin for a moment or so, all eyes upon him. Pointing to two of the younger *oozies*, he said, "Take some food from my stores—enough for three days. Go across the hills to the house of the white Man-of-God. He is also a doctor. Tell him what has happened. Ask him to come as soon as he can. You should be back here in three days. If our master does not improve, we will carry him to meet the Man-of-God. That will save time."

When the two men were almost ready to leave, Ba Thet heard Chaung Thak say to them, "One other thing you will tell the Man-of-God. Say to him that seven or eight men of the Mooser tribe are traveling south and carrying a stock of opium. If word can be got to the police quickly, the men might be caught with the drugs. You know what that will mean!"

The two *oozies* exchanged glances. They knew as well as Chaung Thak that when opium smugglers were caught there was always a police reward. Chaung Thak laughed dryly as if he read their thoughts. "No need to wonder. You will get your share of the reward," he promised. "And go all the quicker for that."

Chaung Thak bustled the rest of the men and boys into rebuilding some of the broken-down huts while he did what he could for Johnson. Chaung Thak's guess about what had happened was absolutely right. The bullet fired by the leader of the Mooser men would have killed Bill Johnson had it not struck the butt of his rifle. The force had smashed the rifle against Johnson's face and forehead, and the blow had been a heavy one.

Two hours before sunset Johnson opened his eyes. Chaung Thak, with Ba Thet to help him, had been putting cold-water compresses on the swollen forehead and face, and they had finally had their effect. A few minutes later Bill Johnson was accepting a mug of strong tea from Chaung Thak and asking for the medicine chest so he could take two aspirins for his headache.

After resting for half an hour, Johnson listened to the story of what had happened, then took the damaged rifle from the old man and examined it.

"It saved my life, I suppose," he said ruefully, looking at the gash torn in the polished wood of the butt. He tried to work the cartridge ejector, and it would not work. The bullet had damaged the mechanism. "That won't fire again until it has been looked at by a gunsmith," he said, handing the weapon back to Chaung Thak.

For several minutes he sat, eyes closed, his face furrowed by a frown of pain. Then Ba Thet, unable to contain his anxiety any longer, asked when they could go back to rescue his uncle.

"The monsoon has not reached our valley yet," Ba Thet said apologetically. "But there will be floods up in the hills, and when they come down to us. . . ." He did not finish his sentence, but Bill Johnson understood.

"Yes, of course, your uncle. We've got to get him out from under those rocks. What about Poo Koon? Is he likely to go off into the jungle?"

"No," Ba Thet assured him quickly. "He does not roam. Just as soon as the pain goes, then he will come back here and all will be well."

"Yes, I've got a feeling Poo Koon won't leave the riverbed," said Johnson. That means that if we take the elephants up to free Sing Noi, he might interfere. Could we keep him off with three or four of our bulls?"

Chaung Thak pondered for a moment before saying, "Elephants are like men. They know if there is something wrong with another elephant. I think they know Poo Koon is mad—and I don't think they will face him."

"Have you ever trapped an elephant in a pit?" Johnson asked. When the old man nodded, he said, "Then that is what we must do. We'll dig a pit near to the rocks where Sing Noi is trapped, and if Poo Koon does come, we'll have to try and lure him into it. I hate doing it—but we can't waste time. Call the men together. I'll have a word with them."

Five minutes later the *oozies* and *paijaiks* were gathered in a silent half circle near the green tent. Chaung Thak brought out a chair, and then Bill Johnson came out and sat down. Half his face was covered with a bandage, and he looked haggard.

"We're going upriver to free Sing Noi," he told them, "but if Poo Koon comes we could be in deep trouble. If we had four or five of the biggest tuskers to act as guards—they might be able to drive him off. He'll fight, of course, but we have got to save Sing Noi—and do it quickly. Now I want volunteers who will bring their tuskers along. Raise your hands, those who will."

Not one hand was raised. The men were sorry for Sing Noi, but worried about their own elephants. An old *oozie* asked, "Who will pay compensation to me for my bull if he is injured? Suppose he is hurt and cannot haul teak again. I am a poor man, and my bull is my only wealth. Poo Koon is very strong, and we think he is mad. A mad tusker is a terrible animal."

Heads nodded to show that the other men who owned elephants were thinking the same thing. Nor could Bill Johnson promise that injured elephants would be paid for. His contract was to get out teak. He was allowed money to hire men and elephants— not to rescue men who were in trouble from some cause other than hauling teak.

Bill Johnson sighed. Obviously he understood how the men felt, but he made an appeal to their feelings for Sing Noi. "I'm going to leave you for a few minutes," he told them. "Think over what I have said. Sing Noi is your friend. Do you not sometimes risk something to help a friend who is in trouble. Think how it would be if *you* were under the rocks instead of Sing Noi."

As he returned to his tent, the *oozies* and *paijaiks* began to rise. They murmured uncomfortably to one another. It was all very well for the white man to talk like that—he did not own an elephant.

Then Ba Thet halted them. His eyes flashed with anger and indignation as he addressed one of the *oozies*. "Tell me, Nga Tun, who was it that brought the Man-of-God across the hills when the monsoon rains were turning everything to water and mud. Your wife had been clawed by a black bear. Everyone thought she would die—only *one man* would walk through the jungle because of the fear of the lame tiger that had killed and eaten some women and children. Do you remember who brought the Man-of-God? Would your wife be living now if he had not come? Who brought the Man-of-God, Nga Tun? Tell me—was it a man named Sing Noi?"

Heads turned and men looked at Nga Tun. He shuffled his feet uneasily, but before he could say anything Chaung Thak laughed sarcastically and pointed to another man. "And who was it that saved your life when a leopard dropped on you from a tree? Was it not this boy's father? And from that day

64

he must stay in his own village because the spotted cat bit his ankle so badly that he cannot now ride his own elephant."

"It is all forgotten now, so no one will help my uncle," Ba Thet said bitterly. "I must go."

"Not so. I will help," Nga Tun broke in, and looking across to a man with scars, he said, "And can you forget that Ba Thet's father saved you?"

In five minutes there were enough volunteers, and Chaung Thak peered into the green tent to tell Bill Johnson that six *oozies* and their elephants were ready to go upriver as soon as the word was given.

"In an hour," Johnson said. "I shall feel better then, and there is less chance of Poo Koon's coming when darkness hides us. Make a meal for everyone, Chaung Thak, and tell the men that there will be a bonus payment for them all when Sing Noi is back in camp."

Everyone was more cheerful by the time the sun went down. Chaung Thak had made a big meal, and added more than the usual amount of spices. That helped. Bill Johnson was also feeling better. He had always kept himself very fit, and though his head probably throbbed painfully, he seemed to be getting over the nasty knock he had sustained.

He spoke lightheartedly to the men as he inspected the chosen elephants and the equipment that was to be taken upriver. There were picks and spades and baskets for carrying earth. Ropes and dragging chains were already up there, lying where they had been dropped when Poo Koon had come and forced the elephants into a hasty retreat.

"I have a feeling that Poo Koon will visit us again," Johnson admitted, when he addressed the men and boys. "Since the rain has not yet got to our valley, we shall not risk trying to clear the rocks off Sing Noi, but will dig a pit to trap the mad bull."

"That is good," said one of the older *oozies*. "Our elephants are uneasy. If Poo Koon did come they might run away—and we would not be able to get them back a third time."

"There is one other thing, Mr. Johnson," said another *oozie*. "We all know Poo Koon. He is not a fool. Will he walk into a pit? I think not."

"I was coming to that," Johnson said, smiling as if getting a pain-maddened tusker to drop into a trap was the easiest thing in the world. "The pit will be dug near the place where Sing Noi waits for rescue. It will be deep—ten feet—and just wide enough to hold this unhappy tusker. He must not have room to fight, or he might break down one of the pit walls and climb out."

Heads nodded in agreement. More than one pit-trapped tusker had got out that way.

"The pit will be covered with light bamboos and maybe some earth to hide it."

"Poo Koon would see it," Ba Thet protested. "I know he would. He will not walk into a trap like that."

"He is going to *run* into it," Johnson said quietly. "Along the middle of the length of the pit there will be a narrow plank—wide enough for a man to put his feet safely, not wide enough for even a clever elephant to walk on. Do you understand?"

Heads nodded, but no one was smiling. They could visualize a pit with a plank running along the middle lengthwise, but could not imagine how Poo Koon could be got to run, actually run, into such a trap. Poo Koon was far too sensible.

"If he does come," Johnson said, "I want one man to go out to meet him. If the bull is still in a killer mood, he will chase the man, who will run straight back toward the pit. He will cross the top of the pit by means of the plank. If Poo Koon is unable to stop, he will fall into the hole. It is a simple plan, and it should work. Once he is trapped we can get on with the work of rescuing Sing Noi without fear of interruption."

He looked around the half circle of men and boys, whose faces were just visible in the light of the dying day. Not one of them had a smile for the white man. Faces were glum.

"I want someone to volunteer who can run well," Johnson said after a long silence, "and there will be a bonus payment of fifty ticals for the man who does the job. Whoever does it will be showing himself to be a real friend of Sing Noi. It is no use trying to dig him out of the rocks until Poo Koon is trapped."

Again there was no response from any of the assembly. "I could shoot Poo Koon with the double-barreled shotgun, but I don't want to do that. I am sure this madness of his will pass away. He is a valuable elephant, and it will be a great loss to Sing Noi and young Ba Thet if the elephant has to be killed. If we can trap him he can be freed later when the danger to Sing Noi is past."

Still there was only silence. Ba Thet stared into the gathering gloom. His heart thumped wildly. What Johnson was asking would be a terrible risk. Over a short distance an angry elephant can run faster than most men, and if Poo Koon caught anyone he would kill him without hesitation. Yet Ba Thet raised his hand. He could not let their elephant be shot.

"I will do it," he said. At once all eyes turned on him and there was a hissing intake of breath at this foolishness.

"There will, of course, be fifty ticals for you, even though Poo Koon is your elephant," Johnson said.

"I do it for my uncle and for Poo Koon," Ba Thet said chokily. "Can we go soon?"

"Now!" Johnson said, and there was a sudden tautness in his voice as he added, "I shall not let you do it, Ba Thet. This is a man's task, not work for a boy. You shall receive fifty ticals—for your courage. But *I* will tempt Poo Koon into the pit." He reached for his pipe, stared into the empty bowl for a moment or so, then said abruptly, "We will leave in five minutes."

A Trap for Poo Koon

AS THE MEN AND BOYS MOVED OFF TO WHERE THE elephants were tethered, Ba Thet turned to Chaung Thak to ask, "Can a man who has been hurt, as Mr. Johnson has been hurt, run faster than an angry bull elephant? He will be caught and killed."

Chaung Thak continued to ladle water into the rice pans for a moment or so. Then he said, "I began to work with white men when I was a *paijaik* forty years ago. Even as a boy I wondered at them. They come to the teak country with white faces, arms, and knees. They are young and eager to learn. Some have fevers and return home; many become old men before their time; but in one thing they are all the same."

"Yes?" Ba Thet said anxiously.

"None has a crooked tongue. When they say they will do a thing—they do it. If Mr. Johnson says he will bring Poo Koon to a pit, that he will do."

Ba Thet shook his head and stared past the old man into the gloom. Away to the north vivid flashes of lightning were searing the sky almost continuously. Up in the hills monsoon rain was already slashing down in torrents. Before long, even if the rain did not reach the Keng Oom Valley, the flood waters from upcountry would.

Bill Johnson could not begin rescue work until he was sure Poo Koon could not interrupt them. It meant digging a deep pit, and that would take time.

Chaung Thak broke into the boy's unhappy thoughts by reminding him that his uncle was probably both hungry and thirsty. They must prepare food for him and fill a bamboo water carrier.

When everyone was ready Bill Johnson checked elephants and equipment. By the light of a lamp he looked at every man and boy. He was dressed in khaki shorts and shirt, but Chaung Thak nudged Ba Thet and motioned at Johnson's feet. He was no longer wearing the heavy boots that were his normal footgear. Now he wore a pair of light rubber shoes.

"You see, boy," the old man whispered. "He thinks of everything. In those shoes he will run like the wind."

It certainly did seem as if Johnson had forgotten nothing. Boys had gone to the nearest brake of bamboo to cut torches. Then they had split and fuzzed out the ends so that they would ignite more quickly. There was a two-gallon can of paraffin. When they started work the boys who carried the torches would dip the fuzzed-out ends in the paraffin. If Poo Koon did come, they could set fire to the torches immediately.

Johnson was taking his double-barreled shotgun, and he had the safety catch in the "off" position. If Poo Koon was still in killer mood, and met them, split seconds would count.

"The elephants and their *oozies* will stay on the bank at the place where they usually go down onto the riverbed," Johnson said. "Once the pit is dug I will send a runner to call them. In that way we will not have the tuskers frightened if Poo Koon does put in an appearance."

He gave the order to leave, and they moved north. They left the elephants at the prearranged spot, and the rest of the party slid down the bank onto the riverbed. They moved in silence and without light. The flashes of lightning showed them the way, for they were now almost continuous as the bad weather moved nearer.

Ba Thet went to his uncle and pushed the food and water-filled bamboo through to him. He told him that rescue preparations were beginning right away.

The moment Bill Johnson had marked out where the pit digging was to begin, he also came to speak a word of cheer to Sing Noi.

"You are too kind," Sing Noi croaked. "I shall remember this until I die."

"So shall I," Johnson murmured as he moved away. He added to Chaung Thak, "I'm just going to keep my fingers crossed and hope Poo Koon keeps away and that the floods don't come to beat us."

Several times through the hours that followed Bill Johnson said he wished he had brought the elephants here instead of digging the pit, for there was no sign of Poo Koon. Adding to their worry was the increasing fury of lightning and thunder overhead. There were several short, sharp showers of rain, yet the first gray of dawn came without any real flooding of the riverbed. The rains wet the mud, but that was all.

When the pit was almost finished Bill Johnson decided to try out his plan for trapping Poo Koon. They laid a long, three-inch-thick plank lengthwise across the middle of the pit, and the diggers climbed out. Silently they stood back to watch.

After testing the strength of the plank Johnson walked about thirty yards away toward the middle of the riverbed. All eyes were on him in the growing light of dawn. Everyone was thinking the same thing, that only a white man would be mad enough to believe he could lure a pain-crazed tusker into a pit. Only a white man could imagine he could run at top speed to the pit and cross the narrow plank.

Yet Bill Johnson did it. Running like a hundred-yards sprinter, he reached the edge of the pit. His right foot hit the teak planking a yard from the edge.

73

It sagged visibly, yet within seconds the test was over and Johnson proved he could do it.

A few minutes later the diggers returned to the pit to clear out the piles of wet mud in the bottom and to make the trap deep enough. Suddenly there came a faint sound from the north, a droning that increased rapidly until it became a thunderous boom.

Within seconds the anxious watchers saw the water arrive. Two hundred yards to the north the riverbed suddenly narrowed and ran for several hundred yards through a defile cut through a rocky hillside. Flood water coming from the hill country was always compressed in that defile before it burst out into the wider riverbed.

The flood came into view as a five-foot-high wall of foam-topped water. There was tremendous pressure behind it, but the sudden widening of the riverbed took much of the power out of it. Long before it reached the edges of the pit its five-foot height had gone, and only a little water spread across to the riverbank itself.

In minutes the flood had gone, but it was a grim warning of what was to come.

"Fetch the elephants," Johnson roared, pointing to a *paijaik* standing nearby. "And tell the *oozies* to do some ear scratching," he added, knowing that an *oozie* scratched behind his tusker's ear with his big toenail when he wanted the elephant to hurry.

The runner went off, but as Bill Johnson took out

his pipe there was a sudden chorus of shouts from the *paijaiks* who had been posted to act as watchers and guards with torches out on the riverbed. "He is here. Poo Koon is coming!"

Every head turned, and in the growing light of day they saw him. He had been resting downstream, and the flood water rushing by had wet him from head to foot. If he had not already seen the watchers, their shouts drew his attention. He turned and began to walk at a good pace in their direction.

Men and boys fled for the safety of the thirty-foot-high riverbank, leaving Bill Johnson to go out and meet the tusker. This was the moment they had planned for. Now they would see whether the white man's trap would work.

Poo Koon walked toward the trap as Bill Johnson advanced to meet him. There would come a moment

when the bull would either respond to Johnson's shout of "*Hmit*" or charge.

Ba Thet, who had been sitting at the foot of the rocks talking to his uncle, saw everything. The rush of flood water had gone, but the stream running down the center of the riverbed was now more than twenty feet wide.

The brightening light of early morning shone white on the water, making the figures of Bill Johnson and the tusker stand out as sharp-cut silhouettes, black against white.

In the excitement of the moment Ba Thet forgot to tell his uncle what was happening, but he was soon reminded when Sing Noi's grip on his hand tightened and the old man asked anxiously, "Why are the men and boys shouting? What is happening? Is more water coming down?"

"Our elephant is coming," Ba Thet said, and dragged his hand from his uncle's grip. Slowly he rose and his heart began to thump as he watched Poo Koon stop, while Bill Johnson continued to walk steadily and without hesitation nearer the big tusker.

In the hope of tempting the tusker to try and catch him off guard, Johnson stopped and stooped as if to retie his shoelace, but he never took his eyes off the tusker. Poo Koon remained motionless, but his big ears lifted a little, a sign that he was as taut-muscled as the man standing before him.

"He should not go nearer," Ba Thet muttered, clenching and unclenching his hands in an agony of fear. "Poo Koon is just waiting for his chance. Please, Mr. Johnson, stay where you are."

Bill Johnson walked a yard or so nearer. Up the valley the clouds thickened and grew darker. The wind was bringing the rains ever closer. If Johnson was to race over the wet mud, he had to do it now before falling rain made the surface even more treacherous. He must make Poo Koon chase him.

Unless he could lure the big tusker over to the pit, the chance to rescue Sing Noi would be gone. If more floods came, the trapped man would drown. Bill Johnson advanced another six yards. Now he was nearly fifty yards from the pit and less than twenty yards from Poo Koon. He dare not go nearer!

Next, Johnson tried shouting insults at Poo Koon, but got no response at all. Then he walked a yard or so to the right and bent to loosen a large stone that lay there in the mud.

As if he had been waiting for just such a move, Poo Koon came to sudden, devastating life. He gave a shrill *rrrrrrmmmmmmmph* and charged. But Johnson was ready. Swinging around he began to run. He held his own for ten yards, but by then Poo Koon had got into his stride and the distance between man and elephant dwindled.

Ba Thet stood upright now, his eyes bulging. Poo Koon was running with his trunk out at full stretch. Little more than a flick of the trunk end might throw Johnson to the ground.

From the men and boys safe on the riverbank

came a chorus of yells of encouragement, shrieks of anger at Poo Koon, and pleas for their white employer to run even faster. Bill Johnson needed no encouragement, for he could hear the *thud-thud-thud* of Poo Koon's big feet behind him, and they seemed even closer than they actually were.

The covered pit was very near now. Johnson had to bound onto the stretch of narrow teak and get over to the far side before the big bull crashed down into the pit.

He bounded onto the plank, his right foot hitting the teak almost halfway along its length. A split second later he skidded sideways. His rubber shoe had come down on a fragment of wet mud. It slithered and his balance was gone. Yells of dismay from the bank above drowned out Johnson's bellow as he made a really fantastic effort to turn in the direction of the skid and leap for the side of the pit. His great effort just failed. His left foot came down on the split bamboo. Strong enough only to bear its own weight and that of a light covering of earth and leaves, the bamboo bent, opened up, and let him through to the pit below.

Ba Thet instinctively closed his eyes, for he had a sudden mental picture of Poo Koon crashing into the pit on top of Johnson. He opened them a moment later when even the horrified shouts of the *oozies* and *paijaiks* on the bank were drowned by a thunderous roar from the big tusker.

He had been seven yards behind Johnson when the trap opened up and swallowed the man. Poo Koon had not been directly in line with the camouflaged pit and he was able to swerve sufficiently to avoid the trap. His impetus carried him on until he was only a few yards from the riverbank itself.

He stared up at the men and boys above him. The bolder among them began screaming abuse at him, and one even picked up a clod of earth and threw it down so that it broke on the tusker's forehead. Bellowing in fury, Poo Koon heaved himself onto his hind feet, his forefeet pawing at the riverbank. With his trunk at full stretch, he tried to reach the yelling figures above him. He was yards away from them, but the *oozies* and *paijaiks* drew back, frightened by his rage. After bringing down a shower of earth with his front feet Poo Koon slowly dropped back onto all fours.

It was then he showed why men called him intelligent. He stared about him for a moment and saw a stone that must have weighed about thirty pounds. Coiling the end of his trunk about it, he lifted the stone and, in one swift movement, hurled it at the yelling figures above him.

Oozies and *paijaiks* retreated out of range, and for a minute or more there was almost silence. The thunder was still muttering to the north, and the lightning was searing the sullen clouds, but when Poo Koon stopped his wild bellowing, it did indeed seem almost quiet.

Ba Thet stood rigid. He was less than fifteen yards from his elephant, and at the least move Poo Koon would be on him. Even Sing Noi seemed to realize that something dreadful had happened, for his whispered pleas to be told what was going on died away.

Slowly the big tusker turned around. His trunk swung this way and that, and Ba Thet could hear the *sssssssssss* as air was sucked in. Poo Koon was testing the air, trying to discover which way Bill Johnson had gone. One moment he had been there and the next he had vanished.

Johnson himself gave his position away. When he crashed through the pliant bamboos covering the pit, he had landed spread-eagled. The bamboo had partially broken his fall, but he was bruised, and worse than that, he had fallen face down into the two inches of soft mud at the bottom of the pit. Johnson sputtered and choked as he spat out the mud and tried to clear his nostrils.

Ba Thet's heart almost stopped beating as he saw Poo Koon swing ponderously around, his ears flapping gently. Though his eyesight might be poor, there was nothing wrong with his hearing or his powers of scent. *Oozies* on the bank began to shout warnings to the dazed Bill Johnson, urging him to keep quiet, but it was already too late.

After staring at the pit, with its disarranged pattern of split bamboos, Poo Koon gave a long suspicious sniff, then slowly walked nearer. As yet he could not see the man below, but after he had coiled his trunk about a section of the bamboo and dragged it clear, Bill Johnson was in plain sight.

Poo Koon stood staring into the ten-foot-deep pit for several seconds, almost as if he could not believe his eyes. Then he gave a deep grunt, out went his trunk again, and seconds later the last remaining lengths of bamboo had either been dragged clear, or had fallen into the pit.

Bill Johnson shouted for help, hastily gathering the bamboos that had fallen into the pit to use as a shield, for Poo Koon had thrust his trunk deep and was trying hard to grab the man below him.

Chaung Thak did what he could. He had retreated some fifty yards upstream and, kneeling so that he could get the best aim possible, he fired the shotgun, aiming at the tusker's rear.

Some of the pellets must have lodged in Poo Koon's buttocks, for he gave a defiant roar, more at the sound of the gun than from pain brought on by the pellets. He lifted his trunk out of the pit for a moment, then changed his mind and, dropping gently to his knees, swept his trunk deep around the bottom. Bill Johnson knelt under some bamboos and fended off the trunk tip, but it could only be a matter of a minute or so before Poo Koon snatched the bamboos away and left Johnson with no protection at all.

Ba Thet watched in an agony of terror. He was frightened, yet something drove him out into the open. He had to do something, and he had to do it at once. If Poo Koon got a trunk-tip grip on Bill Johnson's shirt or shorts, that would be the end of him, for the elephant would haul him up and kill him.

The watching *oozies* and *paijaiks* saw Ba Thet rush to the rescue. Men who had lived with elephants all their lives gaped in astonishment as they saw how the boy tackled the job. Ba Thet ran behind the big tusker, grabbed his tail end, and twisted it with all the power he could command.

Though half crazed with the pain from his broken tusk, and temporarily mad with the lust to kill, Poo Koon's trunk-lashing attack on Bill Johnson stopped. The new pain as his tail was twisted made him heave himself to his feet, squealing even harder than before.

He flicked his tail and swung Ba Thet off his feet. But Ba Thet had expected that twitch, and hung on grimly. He gave the tail a further twist the moment his feet were on the ground again, bringing another prolonged blast of rage and pain from the tusker.

Poo Koon started to turn around, wanting now to find his tormentor. His tail swung again, and this time the twitch was so violent that Ba Thet's grip was broken. He stumbled backward for several yards and then sat down with a thump. By then Poo Koon had turned, and saw him as he began to rise.

Ba Thet Buys Time

"DRAW HIM AWAY! DRAW HIM AWAY!" A DOZEN VOICES screamed the command to Ba Thet. The *oozies* felt that if the boy could lure the tusker away for a few minutes they would be able to scramble down the bank and snatch Johnson out of the pit and to safety.

Ba Thet hardly heard the screaming from above. In the seconds or so between falling backward and getting to his feet again he had only one thought—to get out of Poo Koon's reach. He knew he had hurt the big tusker, and he knew Poo Koon would try to get his revenge.

He had a frightening vision of the huge trunk swinging a few yards away, of the open mouth as Poo Koon screamed with rage; then he started to run. It was no use making for the riverbank. He could never hope to scramble up that thirty-foot height before the tusker reached him. Even if he got halfway up, the long trunk could reach out and pluck him down as a man plucks a ripe mango from its branch.

There was only one way to run, toward the middle of the riverbed. His first thought was that he might gain a few precious seconds by crossing the central stream. Its banks were no more than a foot high, yet even a low step down will make an elephant hesitate. Their weight and bulk make it impossible for them to jump. They are reluctant to step down into a river until they have tested the depth to make sure the ground below water is firm enough for them.

Ba Thet's hopes of gaining ground by crossing the central stream died almost at once. He had not realized that by now much more water was coming down from the hills, and as a consequence the stream had overflowed its banks and was spreading across the main channel. There was now a thirty-foot-wide flood surging along, carrying with it dead branches, clumps of grass, and all the flotsam that a sudden flood snatches from the banks of a river.

Within seconds he was splashing through water an inch or so deep and throwing sheets of spray on either side. Poo Koon followed him, and he could hear the big bull's angry squeals as he splashed into the water.

The hard-baked mud had begun to soften a little, making the surface treacherous, and if Ba Thet had been wearing shoes he would almost certainly have had more trouble than he did. He slipped once, and his heart almost stopped beating in terror as he sensed Poo Koon closing in on him.

Just in time he reached the central channel. He

plunged in and the water came up to his knees. For all his blind rage, Poo Koon must have remembered the stream, for he suddenly slowed down, his trunk dipping into the water until he found the bank. It gave Ba Thet a forty-yard advantage, and he turned to run upstream.

By this time he was panting. The water impeded him more than it did the tusker. In desperation he turned and crossed the stream a second time. Poo Koon followed him, and again lost ground as he trod gingerly down into the deeper water.

Twice more the same trick enabled Ba Thet to keep ahead of Poo Koon, but even so, he soon lost his advantage. The tusker was very strong, and he was driven on by a blind, mad rage.

Yet the elephant was cunning enough to realize that each time he crossed the stream he lost ground. Therefore, when Ba Thet crossed the stream for the third time and headed up river once more, Poo Koon stepped into the deeper water, then turned upstream without climbing up the shallow bank again. Now, if Ba Thet tried to cross the channel, he would gain no advantage. The elephant had outthought him.

Ba Thet was almost on the point of throwing himself down and accepting whatever happened. Panic made his heart thump at a suffocating speed. He was breathless. Poo Koon had gained on him, and the end was very near when out of the narrow valley came the water once more with a roaring, hollow boom.

The wave was a yard high, and it swept out into the wider part of the riverbed with a force that tumbled Ba Thet backward and plunged him along like a matchstick in a flooded gutter. He was carried to within two yards of Poo Koon, but the tusker did not see him. Poo Koon had lifted his head and his trunk as high as he could, knowing what would happen when the flood wave struck him. As Ba Thet swept by, the wave hit the tusker. It was like surf breaking on a rocky shore. There was an explosion of water, and a cloud of spray like a bomb burst hid the huge beast for several seconds.

Half a minute later Ba Thet slid face down along the mud as the water shallowed so rapidly that it could no longer carry him along. The sudden widening of the river at this point always took the sting out of a flood wave, and that had happened now.

Coughing and spluttering, Ba Thet got to his knees. For the moment he was so stunned that he forgot the dangers of a minute earlier. All he wanted was to clear the muddy water from his throat and nostrils and his face and eyelashes.

Sixty yards farther upriver, Poo Koon stared about him in disgruntled surprise. Just before the flood water came he had been within a dozen yards of the boy he had been chasing. Now there was no living thing to be seen. When he was sure the boy was not there he gave a disgusted scream and, turning about, started downstream again.

It was the scream that revealed the boy to the tusker. Ba Thet, on his knees and wiping his eye-lashes clear of mud, heard the sound and scrambled to his feet, thinking Poo Koon was near. The sudden movement attracted the tusker's attention, and a moment later he lumbered through the shallows toward the boy.

Ba Thet was tired and breathless, but the sight of the tusker bearing down on him gave new strength to his tired legs. Turning, he started to run down-river. By now the water had drained away until there was less than an inch covering the mud. Nearer the bank there was none, and Ba Thet turned that way for safer running. A slip on wet mud could mean death.

Twenty yards from the bank he turned downriver again. There was no chance to make that thirty-foot climb. He ran sixty yards . . . eighty! He was tiring quickly now, and Poo Koon was gaining, though even he was not running at his earlier speed.

Desperately Ba Thet looked about him for some-thing that would give him a chance to escape. There was nothing. The broken-down bank, with its boulders and the deep pit, was forty yards farther on. He was finished. He knew he could not keep on much longer, and the *thud-thud-thud* of Poo Koon's feet behind him seemed very near now.

Then a *paijaik* on the riverbank gave Ba Thet fresh hope, and kept him running when his legs felt like lead and his heart seemed about to burst. The boy was screaming, "Ba Thet! Run! There is a rope let down over the riverbank a little farther on. Mr. Johnson has been rescued and Chaung Thak is there with the gun. He will fire when you get to the rope. Hurry!"

Hurry! Ba Thet splashed wearily on through the film of water on the river mud. Fear kept him going, though every breath he took seemed to draw a coarse file across his lungs. Panic gripped him. He waited now for the terrifying shock of a blow from Poo Koon's trunk.

The elephant was not far behind him. He could vaguely hear Poo Koon puffing. Even the lust to kill could not keep the elephant at full speed. He ran best over short distances, and this chase had already exceeded half a mile. Part of that distance had been in and out of the middle channel, which had sapped even Poo Koon's great strength. He was slowing down, but not as much as Ba Thet.

From the riverbank came a chorus of shouts now, from *oozies* and *paijaiks.* They all seemed to think that Ba Thet did not realize how close Poo Koon was. "He's nearly on you! Hurry! Ba Thet, hurry or he'll get you!"

Then the chorus changed as men and boys all tried to repeat the same thing: there was a rope hanging down the bank. If he got it they could drag him to safety in a second. He splashed on, somehow forcing his leaden legs to lift his feet up and let them down again.

Then he heard the deeper voice of Bill Johnson, bellowing a command that rose easily above the other voices. "Turn right," he called. "Turn right!"

Ba Thet turned right. He hardly knew what he was doing. He was running, and Poo Koon was behind him. Their elephant was going to catch and kill him.

Then, so suddenly it made him forget everything else, he saw the pit they had dug. It was there, in front of him—only a few yards away.

He swerved, and slipped on the wet mud. For one terrifying second he could see the dark rectangle to his left—a vast black opening. Neither bamboo nor teak plank covered any part of it. Ba Thet made a supreme effort to avoid going into the pit. Calling on his last reserves of strength, he leaped across the corner. One foot slid into the pit, but the other stayed on the mud. He skidded, clawed desperately, and hauled himself clear. Then he flopped flat.

He heard Poo Koon's shrill squeal of triumph; he heard, too, the shouts of horror from the men and boys on the bank thirty feet above him—but he was unable to do anything. Every ounce of strength had been drained from him.

91

Flood Water

POO KOON SAW ONLY THE BLACK, RECTANGULAR PIT
when the boy ahead of him fell flat in the mud. Too
late the big tusker realized the danger. His scream of
triumph suddenly cut short, he tried to turn, as Ba
Thet had turned. Like a juggernaut he slid on. His
great feet ploughed into the softening mud. His legs
were stiff, and he dropped the end of his trunk to
the mud, trying to use it as a lever to push himself
to one side. He was too late. Nothing he did would
stop his great weight.

His forefeet slid over the edge of the pit and he
began to drop. He lifted his head and trunk, making
the air quiver with a wail of terror. He knew he was
falling, and a moment later his hind feet also slid
over the edge and he went heavily into the ten-foot
pit.

The impact as his tremendous weight struck the
bottom of the pit made the riverbed quake for yards

around, and stilled the clamor of voices from the top of the bank. The men and boys should have been glad, but they were elephant lovers and the sight of the big bull plunging down with such a terrific thud silenced them all.

Ba Thet knew something had happened, but he was half fainting from terror and exhaustion, and could think of only one thing—to get his hands onto the back of his head and protect himself even a little. He was waiting for Poo Koon's trunk to grab him.

He was still spread-eagled on the mud when the first of the *oozies* reached him. Men and boys came slithering down the thirty-foot bank, yelling in excitement and relief. It was a great moment for them all. Poo Koon was trapped, and they crowded around Ba Thet, congratulating him on his courage and cleverness.

Bill Johnson realized how shocked Ba Thet was and brushed them aside. "Leave him," he ordered. He took Ba Thet by the arm and gently drew him over to a boulder where he could sit down. There he took out his handkerchief, sodden though it was with rain water, and wiped the mud from Ba Thet's face.

"You did a wonderful job, Ba Thet," he said, "and now that Poo Koon is out of the way we'll be able to get on with releasing your uncle."

Mention of the tusker made Ba Thet rise and look across to the pit. *Oozies* and *paijaiks* were back at a respectful distance, looking at Poo Koon. The big tusker stood very quietly. Like Ba Thet he was suffering from shock. The fall into the deep pit had given him a severe shaking, and he might well have fallen if the pit walls had not given him support.

"Don't worry about him," Johnson said, forcing Ba Thet to sit down again. "Rest. The elephants will be here soon to move the rocks, and I'll want you to sit as close to Sing Noi as you can while we are doing that. He'll need someone to reassure him when the rocks move."

The gray of dawn was turning to full morning now, though there was still no sign of the sun. Leaden clouds covered the sky—the monsoon was here with a vengeance. The stream that had flowed quietly down the center of the riverbed the previous day was now swollen to a sixty-foot flood.

Bill Johnson frowned deeply as he looked across the water to the far bank. Ba Thet knew what he was thinking. Farther north, in the hills, torrential showers of rain had been falling continuously throughout the night. Very soon the river would spread right across to both banks. It would be deepening all the time. If they were to get Sing Noi out alive it would have to be done within the next hour.

Turning to the nearest *oozie*, Johnson said, "Go and see what's happened to the runner I sent off. He should have been back now with the elephants."

The *oozie* stared at Johnson, his eyes widening. Then he turned to look across at the little clusters of men and boys. They, too, had heard the command, and their chatter died away. Suddenly, they all looked scared, and for a few moments the only sounds came from the river and the rain now drumming on the mud.

"Well, what are you waiting for?" Johnson demanded angrily.

"Sir. . . ." The *oozie* somehow got the one word out, but before he could say anything else a quaking *paijaik* was pushed out of a little group toward Johnson. In a terror-filled voice the boy muttered, "Sir . . . I . . . I was the one you told to fetch the tuskers. I was going when Poo Koon came onto the riverbed. I stopped to watch what happened. Then I forgot your orders. Sir, I. . . ." In abject terror the boy sank to his knees and laid his hands on Bill Johnson's feet.

People said of Johnson that he never lost his temper. That was what made him so beloved by those who worked for him. At the moment, however, he seemed to lose his usual iron control. The muscles of his right arm tensed and his fist bunched. The frightened boy at his feet had probably never been nearer a thrashing.

Thrusting his right hand deep into the pocket of his bush jacket, Bill Johnson ordered the trembling boy to his feet. In a voice that sounded strange to the awed listeners he said slowly, "Fetch the elephants now—and hurry. What you forgot to do may cost Sing Noi his life."

"Yes, sir!" Leaping to his feet the *paijaik* turned and ran, with the desperate speed that comes from terror.

No one spoke. Even the youngest *paijaik* knew that before very long there would be deep water spreading from one bank of the river to the other. Two small waves of water had come down. Very soon there would be an almost continual flood pouring out of the narrow valley, and once that began the river mud would quickly be covered to a depth of several feet.

Upcountry every runnel would be overflowing from the monsoon rains, which had lashed down through the hours of darkness. The beginning of every monsoon season was the same. Had it not been so then teak logging could not have been successful. It needed these swift, short-lived floods to wash the heavy logs of teak downstream to the main river.

Johnson looked for a moment at the tiny gap in the rubble through which they would have to drag Sing Noi when the elephants came. He placed a hand on Ba Thet's shoulder. Then they both turned and looked toward the pit. Poo Koon was recovering. The giant tusker had lifted his trunk and was waving the tip to and fro above the pit, as if trying to find something to get a grip on. Given half a chance, he would fight for his freedom.

In those moments Johnson and Ba Thet were thinking the same thing. They had accomplished what had seemed impossible: got Poo Koon safely trapped. And they had the wire ropes and the dragging chains in position. Only the tuskers were not here!

Ba Thet stared ahead with unseeing eyes. Bill Johnson stalked to and fro, watched by the silent *oozies* and *paijaiks*. Finally Johnson turned to Ba Thet. "Go and speak to your uncle," he said. "He will feel better if you are with him. Tell him everything is ready, and when the elephants arrive we'll have him free within twenty minutes."

As Ba Thet rose there came a sudden burbling roar from the pit. Poo Koon, who had been very badly shaken by his ten-foot drop, had made no sound since. Now he had got his wind back entirely and had started to struggle to get out. With his one undamaged tusk he dug furiously at the mud wall in front of him. If he could dig at it long enough he might be able to scramble out.

Oozies and *paijaiks* watched in silence. The pit was deep, but this tusker was a very determined animal.

"He won't get out," Bill Johnson assured them.

Johnson's words sent a sudden chill through Ba Thet's heart. *He won't get out!* It was like hearing a sentence of death passed on their elephant. Poo Koon *couldn't get out!* Ba Thet closed his eyes for a moment in sick horror at the thought.

He could guess what the end would be. When the

rising water covered the whole of the riverbed, the pit would flood. Gradually the water would rise about Poo Koon—rise until it was over his head. He would not die at once, for he could lift his trunk above the water level and breathe that way. After a few hours, however, exhaustion would bring the trunk tip down. It would slide beneath the muddy water. Then Poo Koon would drown.

"Go on, talk to your uncle," Bill Johnson urged. Turning Ba Thet away from the pit, he gave him a gentle push.

There was nothing he or anyone else could do for the tusker. He was in the pit, and no one could get him out. They could not dig him out, for in his present ugly temper Poo Koon would kill anyone who went near enough to try and dig the mud away.

Ba Thet went over to crouch on the rocks just level with the gap through which his uncle could thrust his hand and forearm. They talked about the rising water, and Sing Noi gave a deep sigh when he heard that Poo Koon was trapped in a pit.

"He will drown," Sing Noi said quietly. "I am sad for that. He was the best elephant born in the country—and he would have been ours after the pay day."

Ba Thet could only sit and gulp, with tears swimming in his eyes. "The elephants will be here soon," he said finally. "Then they will drag the big boulder off the teak log, and when that is done, a tusker will be able to lift the log, and you will be free."

98

"The elephants will not do it," Sing Noi said.

Ba Thet stared into the darkness of the hole. He could just make out the vague outlines of his uncle's face. "The elephants *will* do it, my uncle," he insisted, and even as he waited for a reply there was a sudden commotion from the groups of men and boys waiting for the arrival of the tuskers.

Ba Thet rose and tried to see what was happening. For a moment everything seemed to be the same, except that the *oozies* and *paijaiks* and Bill Johnson, who had been looking down to where they expected to see the elephants, were now all staring toward midstream.

For a moment or so Ba Thet could see nothing to explain their sudden anxiety or the strained expression on Bill Johnson's face. Then he saw a small tree floating in midstream. It should have been rushing along with the current, but instead it was slowly turning around and around and actually moving back upstream.

Something else was happening, too. A few minutes earlier the water rushing downstream had been sixty feet or so in width. Now it was eighty feet. Because the water was no longer flowing downstream it was beginning to spread across the riverbed.

Ba Thet had seen this happen before many times. Somewhere downstream there was a logjam. It was an occurance that teak men expected whenever the monsoon floods came.

The sudden rise of water in the river always lifted the stacked teak logs off the mud and started to carry them downstream. In this clutter of logs there might be one or sometimes several that would swing awkwardly at a narrow place. Then the heavy butt end of a log might drive deep into the riverbank or lodge against a rock. In a matter of minutes, as other logs became tangled with it, these great balks of timber, driven by the flood, would jam themselves in every direction and form a barrier.

Then the debris that the floods always brought down—the masses of dead *kaing* grass, the small trees and broken branches, the chunks of earth washed from the riverbank—would lodge among the logs, and the result would be a dam that would hold back the water.

Unless the logjam was broken up very quickly the water pouring down from the hills backed up and formed a lake upstream. That was what was happening now. At ordinary times it worried no one. Men and elephants often risked their lives below a logjam, trying to drag out the key log. When they managed that the whole structure collapsed, and thousands of tons of water and many hundreds of heavy logs then went rushing downstream in a thundering medley of noise, with *oozies* and *paijaiks* cheering them on their way.

This time it was different. Ba Thet raced across to where Bill Johnson was chewing at his pipe stem and staring across the river, his face screwed up into a worried frown.

"Mr. Johnson," Ba Thet pleaded, tugging anxiously at his shirt sleeve. "The river! Do you see? It is spreading. Soon it will be here, and rising up to my uncle. Unless we free him quickly. . . ."

At that moment the boy who had been sent to bring the elephants and their *oozies* came running up breathlessly. "Mr. Johnson," he gasped, "Gya Po Yin has taken the tuskers downstream. There is a very bad logjam."

"All right," Johnson snapped. "I want everyone downriver. The men who—"

And there Ba Thet interrupted him. He would never have dared interrupt the teak wallah at any other time. Now, however, he was desperate, and his face showed the dismay he felt at what he thought was going to happen. "Sir, you are going to leave my uncle?"

"Look, Ba Thet," Bill Johnson said quietly, "there are two ways to rescue Sing Noi. One is the way I first planned—to get the elephants here and drag the rocks off him. I had thought to do that easily before the river flooded. The other way, and it is the only way now, is to go downriver and break the logjam so the water level will fall."

Ba Thet gulped, but said nothing. He just looked at Johnson, and his eyes spoke volumes.

"We cannot get the elephants here in time," Bill

Johnson went on soberly. "You heard what was said. Gya Po Yin is a good teak man, and he thought it would be my wish that the logjam be broken. So he has taken the elephants downriver. We couldn't possibly get them back in time."

"And my uncle?" Ba Thet said with a quaver in his voice.

"I am going down to break the logjam," said Bill Johnson with a forced smile. "When I do that the water will stop creeping nearer to Sing Noi. We *shall* do it. When the water is running freely again, then we will come back here and get Sing Noi out of his prison."

"Yes—sir," Ba Thet faltered.

"Don't you trust me?" Bill Johnson asked, still managing a little smile. "I shall do my utmost to save Sing Noi."

Ba Thet nodded.

"Now go and sit with your uncle. Tell him not to be afraid. We shall free the jammed logs, then come back here. Try not to worry. Everything will come out all right."

"Yes, sir." The words came out mechanically. Ba Thet knew that Johnson would do his best, but it was hard to believe that everything would "come out all right." The *oozies* and the *paijaiks* were already more than a hundred yards away. The tuskers, for whom the dragging ropes had been laid out in readiness, had moved downriver. If the river continued to rise they could not possibly get back in time to move the rocks and free Sing Noi.

Bill Johnson patted Ba Thet on the shoulder, then sprinted after the *oozies* and *paijaiks*. Ba Thet knew only a miracle could save his uncle now. It would have been difficult enough if the elephants had come upriver the way they had planned. There was only a chance in a thousand that they could break the log-jam in time. If it was a bad jam, as the *paijaik* had said, then it became a chance in a million.

Ba Thet stared at Johnson's retreating figure, then looked at the river. The water was so near now that some of it was trickling into the pit where Poo Koon fought to dig his way to freedom. But the tusker was now silent. It seemed as if he, too, realized that time was running out.

A voice made Ba Thet turn, startled. It was the old man, Chaung Thak. He had not gone off with the others.

"This is a sad day, Ba Thet." He was shaking his head as he spoke. "In half the time it takes to boil rice, they will both be dead. And there is nothing we can do—nothing."

Two to Die?

BA THET SWALLOWED THE LUMP IN HIS THROAT. HE blinked desperately to keep back the tears that threatened to flow down his cheeks, and turned away. To see their mighty tusker down in that muddy pit fighting for his life and not be able to help was a terrible thing. Even more terrible would be to sit and talk to his uncle while the river water flowed nearer and nearer, bringing death to the man who, next to his father, he loved best of all.

The rain hissed down as Ba Thet sank to a crouching position on the rocks. He thrust his right arm through the gap and a moment later felt Sing Noi grip his hand. He was still there, still waiting.

Ba Thet could not think of anything to say, and he was glad when Chaung Thak joined them. Thrusting his face as close to the gap in the rocks as he could, the older man called in, "This is a bad day for us, Sing Noi. Has Ba Thet told you that there is a logjam downriver? It is making the water rise very quickly."

Ba Thet felt his uncle's grip on his hand tighten for a moment. A moment later, in a voice that was determinedly calm, his uncle said, "He has not told me, Chaung Thak, but my nephew is far too kind to give me such bad news. You are telling me that I shall soon drown. Is that it, my old friend?"

"It is better to know the truth and so be prepared," Chaung Thak said soberly. "If there was anything we could do we would do it, but that fool Gya Po Yin has taken the tuskers downriver to the logjam. They should have come here to set you free. So . . . what can we do? An old man and a sixteen-year-old boy!"

"And what about our elephant?" Sing Noi asked. "Is he free? I have not heard him bellowing for the past little while."

Ba Thet looked anxiously at Chaung Thak, but the older man believed in telling the truth.

"I said this was a bad day for us, Sing Noi. You know we dug a pit for Poo Koon. He is in that pit, and it is beginning to fill with water. He cannot get out."

Ba Thet heard his uncle give a deep sigh, but after a moment or so he said, "Chaung Thak, we must do something for him. Twenty-five years ago I saw Poo Koon an hour after he was born. I said to my younger brother who is Ba Thet's father, 'One day we will buy this elephant.' Even when he was a little *butcha*, I could see that he would grow into a mighty tusker. Now, if he is to die, we should make it easy for him. I would not like him to die in pain or fear. What can you do, old friend?"

Chaung Thak and Ba Thet exchanged glances. Both looked back to the pit where Poo Koon was still digging frantically and making little headway. His single tusk dug into the damp mud in the wall of the pit, made a hole, but came out again without getting him any nearer to freedom.

"What *can* we do, my uncle?" Ba Thet finally asked, when it seemed Chaung Thak was not going to speak. "We cannot go near him. His eyes are still red with the madness. *You* know elephants—tell us what we can do."

"There is a way," was the quiet reply, and Sing Noi's listeners were startled to hear him chuckle.

"How can you laugh when you and your elephant face death?" Chaung Thak asked.

"I laugh not about the elephant or myself," Sing Noi replied, his voice more sober. "I laugh to think that the Mooser men, who were responsible for my being here, and who made Poo Koon break his tusk, left something behind to help us."

Chaung Thak and Ba Thet exchanged anxious glances. The same thought had occurred to both of them: the strain of being held prisoner under the great heap of rock and rubble had made Sing Noi so giddy that he did not know what he was saying.

"That is a strange thing to say," said Chaung Thak.

"No, it isn't. Do you realize I am lying close to so much opium that it would make a man rich if he could sell it?" said Sing Noi.

Again Chaung Thak and Ba Thet exchanged a swift glance. They both knew opium eating or smoking was a crime. Using the drug was punishable in the teak camps by instant dismissal. It clouded men's minds, and more than one *oozie* had been killed by his elephant when he was befuddled by opium.

Ever since he was a small boy Ba Thet had been warned against the drug. He knew that the yard-high poppies from which it was obtained grew thickly in the fields of the upland villages. He knew the dark-brown stuff was smuggled south to the city of Bangkok. One thing his father had always impressed on him was that only a fool used opium.

"What has opium to do with Poo Koon?" Chaung Thak asked harshly.

Again Sing Noi laughed. "I will pass some through to you," he replied. "Give it to my elephant; then he can forget his pain and his fear of death. Here, my nephew, take this."

Ba Thet felt something being pressed into his hand, fitting comfortably in his palm. It was a ball of opium. He looked at Chaung Thak, who shrugged and murmured, "It is your uncle's wish. Perhaps it can help the tusker. You can try it."

Ba Thet rose and looked uneasily at the ball of tacky brown stuff in his hand. He had heard so many stories of what the drug could do that he was afraid of it. Yet when he looked across to the pit where Poo Koon was still struggling to get free he knew he simply had to try something.

While he and Chaung Thak had been talking to Sing Noi, water had spread across the bed of the river. It was creeping in little runnels right up to the riverbank. One tiny stream had reached the pit and was flowing in. Poo Koon was already standing in more than two feet of water, and the level was rising rapidly.

"Don't give him the whole lump," Chaung Thak advised him. "That would be too much even for a big tusker. Give him a piece about the size of a man's thumb. If that is not enough, then you can give him more."

"How do I give it to him?" Ba Thet asked, walking slowly toward the pit, and breaking off a piece of the opium. He rolled the piece into a ball, then stood staring at their elephant, undecided what to do.

Poo Koon had seen him, and had stopped digging his tusk into the mud wall of his prison. He stared at Ba Thet, but the moment the boy took another step forward the big tusker made the air vibrate with a roar of almost maniacal rage. Fortunately, he could not rise up on his hind legs, for the pit was only just long enough for his big form. It was a tight fit, absolutely right for keeping him a prisoner.

Ba Thet called out, "What is the matter with you, you old fool? Be quiet. I am trying to help you. Listen to me. Am I not your *paijaik* who gives you salt and sweetened rice cakes? Open your mouth for medicine."

Poo Koon watched him in silence. After that first terrible roar he had subsided, and now he was staring at the boy over the edge of the pit. Ba Thet came nearer, the opium pill ready in his right hand.

"Open your mouth," Ba Thet coaxed, "and when you have taken this you will forget the pain of your broken tusk."

Poo Koon remained sullenly silent, but when Ba Thet had moved a yard nearer he lifted his long trunk and swept it around in a swinging attempt to knock the boy off his feet. If Ba Thet had not been expecting such a move, he might have had both legs broken.

"Let me try," Chaung Thak suggested, and immediately he leaped back as a spray of thick black mud spattered him from head to foot. Poo Koon was not in the mood to listen to anyone.

"Devil!" the old man roared, wiping the mud from his face and shirt front. "I should have known that if Ba Thet could not get near you it was foolish of me to try. You are too clever by half, and it won't do you any good." He shook his fist at the big tusker;

then, turning to Ba Thet, he said, "The only way you'll get the opium into him is by waiting until he opens his mouth, then tossing it in. Even so, he won't swallow it. He always was too clever to take medicine."

Ba Thet nodded. He remembered a time past when Poo Koon needed a pill. Knowing how difficult he was, Bill Johnson had carefully slit a banana lengthwise, inserted the pill in the middle, then put the two halves of the banana together again.

It had been almost impossible to see that the banana had been slit open; yet when Poo Koon was given the fruit he laid it on the ground, pushed at it for a few seconds with the tip of his trunk, then carefully slid the top half of the split banana off the other portion. The pill was there, for all to see.

Poo Koon had eaten the top half of the banana. He then scraped the pill off the other half and gently rolled it in the direction of Bill Johnson. There was a gleam of amusement in his eyes. Poo Koon was laughing at them. It was as if he had known all the time that they were trying to dose him.

There was a different kind of gleam in the tusker's bloodshot eyes now as Ba Thet again came closer to the edge of the pit. Poo Koon's trunk was coiled; it was like a deadly spring, ready to be uncoiled when the moment was ripe.

Ba Thet could just see into the pit where the water had now risen midway up the elephant's body.

With every minute that passed the chance of doing something for Poo Koon faded.

"I have something good for you," Ba Thet coaxed, halting when he was sure he was just out of reach of the tusker's trunk. "Open your mouth, and don't try any of your tricks or I'll cane your big backside. Do you hear? I'll cane your backside." He repeated the phrase because he often used it to Poo Koon. It was a joke between them.

In the past he had followed the good-humored threat by slapping Poo Koon on the buttocks, a blow that did no more than tickle him. Then the big head would go up and Poo Koon would gurgle with pleasure, for Ba Thet then gave him some special tidbit.

Ba Thet had his right hand ready now, with the pellet of opium in his palm. As a last resort he called on Poo Koon to whistle. It was a trick he had taught the tusker, for which Poo Koon was always rewarded with a special treat. To produce the whistle Poo Koon would throw his head back and point his tusks straight at the sky. Ba Thet hoped that if the tusker did that now he might get a chance to toss the opium down his throat.

Poo Koon stared sullenly at Ba Thet as he called on him over and over again to whistle. He made no sound or movement, but kept his eyes fixed on the boy.

"Watch him," came a warning from the anxious Chaung Thak. And even as the warning was given,

Poo Koon screamed and his trunk uncoiled. It swept across the top of the pit, once more sending black mud flying in all directions.

Ba Thet had seen the sudden narrowing of the tusker's eyes before the effort was made, and he jumped. The trunk swept beneath his feet. Realizing he had failed again, Poo Koon roared. His mouth opened wide and Ba Thet tossed the opium.

He was unlucky, missing his target by the merest fraction. The pill struck the tusker's lower lip and bounced off into the muddy water.

"I'm going to throw a stone at him," Chaung Thak yelled. "Get some more opium ready. Have I worked with elephants all my life to be defeated by one like him?"

He turned and picked up two fairly large stones off the foot of the pile behind him. While he was doing that, Ba Thet broke off another piece of opium and worked it into a ball.

"Be ready," Chaung Thak warned, and a moment later a stone sang through the air and bounced lightly on Poo Koon's forehead. It brought a roar of anger from him, and he lifted his head, opening his mouth as he did so.

It was a chance that might not occur again. Ignoring the risk from the powerful trunk, Ba Thet leaped forward and tossed the opium straight into the open mouth. He almost paid for his daring with his life, for Poo Koon swung his trunk around with astonishing

speed, and the tip smashed down on the mud at the boy's heels as he made a wild leap to one side.

Mud flew everywhere as Chaung Thak came forward, tossing another stone at the big tusker and screaming abuse at him. Not content with that, he scooped up two handfuls of mud and flung them at Poo Koon, plastering his big forehead with the stuff and making the big tusker more furious than ever.

Shaking mud from his hands, Ba Thet turned and shouted, "He's taken the pill. I tossed it right into his mouth." Then as Chaung Thak continued to throw mud at the elephant, Ba Thet lost his temper. He pushed the older man to one side, yelling, "There's no need to torture him. He's taken the opium. I threw it into his mouth."

"Out of the way," Chaung Thak roared, scooping up more mud and flinging it at Poo Koon's head. "I'm not doing this for fun. I want to keep him bellowing at me."

In a sudden blind rage, Ba Thet charged at the old man and flung him flat on the mud. It was bad enough for their elephant to be a prisoner in the pit with no hope of escape, but for Chaung Thak to take advantage of his helplessness was more than Ba Thet could stand. He glared down at the old man, his fists clenched. He was quite ready to use force if Chaung Thak tried to resume his mud throwing.

Chaung Thak returned his glare, then heaved himself into a sitting position and began to scrape the mud off his arms. Grimly he snapped, "You are like every other *paijaik*. When you are sixteen you think you know everything about elephants. By the time you are sixty you will not be so sure. You think because you threw the opium into Poo Koon's mouth that he swallowed it?"

That made Ba Thet doubt and he turned to look toward the tusker. Poo Koon was still bawling angrily and swishing mud off the end of the pit top with his trunk. Looking down at the old man, Ba Thet asked sulkily, "What do you mean I think I know everything. I never said I did. But I know one thing: I am not going to let you throw mud at our elephant just because he can't hit back. You wouldn't dare do it if he was free."

Chaung Thak got to his feet. He wiped the clinging mud from the back of his legs, a look of disgust on his face. Then, with a tired little grin, he said, "I wasn't taking advantage of your tusker, boy. I was trying to keep him so mad that he wouldn't have time to taste the opium and spit the stuff out. That's all I was doing. I just hope he did swallow it, that's all."

Ba Thet's shoulders sagged. Wearily he said, "I am a fool. Let us sit down. You are right about people of sixteen. I should have known that a man of your age would be too wise to waste time throwing mud at an elephant just for the fun of it."

He scraped mud off the back of Chaung Thak's

threadbare khaki jacket, then they both sat down and watched in silence as the water crept nearer and nearer.

It was Chaung Thak who broke the long silence. "One thing I know, Ba Thet: Mr. Johnson has not been able to break the logjam. Look at the pit. The water is up to Poo Koon's mouth now. In a few minutes he will be submerged."

Ba Thet nodded. He bent to pull a shovel away from the water, for it was beginning to sink into the mud, which was now turning to a black slime as the water soaked into it.

He threw the shovel behind him, then turned at the ring of metal on metal. The shovel had struck one of the dragging chains laid out earlier for the rescue attempt, but never used. For a moment Ba Thet stared at the chain, then his eyes lit up as an idea occurred to him. Perhaps there was a chance after all for them to save Poo Koon.

"Chaung Thak," he said, scrambling to his feet. "We *can* save Poo Koon. I know we can. Come on."

"Save him? How?" Chaung Thak got to his feet slowly. He was an old man, and he had done more walking about during the past sixteen hours than for many a long day. He was tired, and his muscles ached.

"I'm going to dig a slope at the end of the pit," Ba Thet said, the words almost tumbling out in his eagerness. "Look, the dragging chains are all ready.

If we can get an end to Poo Koon and give him only half a chance, he will haul himself to safety."

Chaung Thak shook his head and muttered, "I wish we could, boy, but you are forgetting something. The moment you go near the edge of that pit, your tusker will break your ribs in with one blow from his trunk. No, you can't do it. He wouldn't let you."

Ba Thet scrambled across the stones to the shovel. "I'm going to try," he said. "I'm not going to let him drown without doing something. I just can't!"

The Jungle Spirits
Are Winning!

"BE CAREFUL," CHAUNG THAK WARNED AS BA THET cautiously approached the end of the pit. "He may be waiting for his chance."

"No he isn't," Ba Thet called back. "The water is almost up to his eyes, and he isn't even struggling." He stood looking at their elephant from a distance of four yards. Poo Koon had his head thrown back a little, for the level of the water in the pit was now so high that if he had not done that his eyes would have been under water.

"I'm coming to help you," Ba Thet called. "Poo Koon . . . it is Ba Thet, your *paijaik*."

The big eyes blinked slowly, but the tusker made no other sign that he had heard or seen Ba Thet. A moment later Chaung Thak came nearer, and there was a hint of excitement in his voice as he yelled, "Maybe the opium is working. Go nearer, but be ready to jump. If he hits you once, it'll finish you."

Ba Thet's heart was thumping as he advanced another yard. Now he was just about as near as he dare go without getting within reach of Poo Koon's trunk tip. He spoke again, and again the eyes blinked. The big tusker had heard him, but there was none of the lunatic lunging and screaming of twenty minutes earlier.

Nervously Ba Thet dug his spade into the mud, never taking his eyes off the elephant. Nor did Poo Koon take his gaze off the boy; his eyes maintained an unblinking stare.

Ba Thet dug out one spadeful of mud, then a second. Still there was neither sound nor movement from the big tusker.

Taking his courage in both hands, Ba Thet moved nearer to the edge of the pit. He was ready to jump at the least movement. If Poo Koon attacked him now he would be lucky to escape with his life. Two more spadefuls were dug out and then Poo Koon lifted his trunk. Ba Thet dropped his shovel and flung himself to one side, but instead of giving a vicious, swinging blow, the trunk went slowly straight up. Then Poo Koon blew air, making an odd whistle. Ba Thet had spent many hours teaching him that trick.

Face down in the mud, Ba Thet waited; then Poo Koon whistled a second time, and hardly daring to believe what he had heard, Ba Thet scrambled to his feet. He looked at the big tusker, and knew that the unexpected miracle had happened. For some reason, perhaps because the opium was dulling his pain, Poo Koon's madness had left him. Even his eyes had lost their maniacal glitter.

Chaung Thak could see the difference, too, and risked coming closer. When Poo Koon still remained quiet, the old man went for a shovel, and the two of them dug with a fury that soon began to show results. A steep slope two yards wide began to lead into the pit.

Chaung Thak suggested they shovel the mud into the pit, in the hope that it would provide a footing for the tusker, but Ba Thet disagreed with the suggestion.

"Stones would be better," he panted. "The mud will only turn to slime when it gets into the water. You fetch stones while I keep on digging. I'm sure he's sinking lower. I think he keeps moving his feet, and that's digging holes for them in the pit bottom."

Ba Thet was right. The water was softening the mud at the bottom of the pit, and Poo Koon's movements and his great weight had combined to sink him another three inches.

No one could have worked harder than the old man and the young *paijaik*, but it was a losing battle. The logjam was still holding and the continuous flood pouring down from the hills was turning the riverbed into a deepening lake.

Poo Koon was forced to raise his trunk high so that he could breathe. Finally the water reached both banks of the river, and when it did the pit filled to the brim. The water lapped up to Poo Koon's forehead, then gradually covered it completely. After that the only sign that there was an elephant under the water was his long trunk. It waved gently to and fro like the neck of some huge gray-black swan.

Finally Ba Thet and the old man had to admit defeat. They were almost too weary to stand, and when they stopped digging they heard shouts from Sing Noi. The water had reached up to the rocks and seeped in to him.

In a last desperate attempt to save the elephant, Ba Thet hauled the end of one of the dragging chains across to the now invisible pit. He made a loop in the links and tried to get it over the slowly waving trunk. It was no use. Poo Koon did not seem to realize that he was being offered a chance of escape, and after two or three minutes Ba Thet was forced to let it splash down into the muddy water.

"We have done all we can," Chaung Thak said, taking Ba Thet by the arm. "Come, let us go and comfort your uncle. He has been shouting to us for some time."

Heartbroken at having failed to rescue their elephant, Ba Thet went with the old man. The scene on the river had changed completely during the time they had been digging. Now no mud was visible at all. The logjam downstream had finally turned the wide riverbed into a vast lake.

"Where is Mr. Johnson?" Sing Noi asked, grabbing at his nephew's hand the moment it was pushed through the gap in the rocks. "Why are you doing nothing to get me out?"

"Doing nothing!" Ba Thet could have wept at the injustice of that remark. He ached from head to foot. No one could have worked harder.

But his uncle, now half frantic with fear and gripping Ba Thet's hand until it hurt, shouted, "You told me they were going to break the logjam and set the water free. Why haven't they done that? The water is here. I can feel it coming up and up."

"The jam must have been a very bad one, old friend," Chaung Thak called in gently. "It is taking longer than we thought."

"You mean they *cannot* break it," Sing Noi wailed.

"They *will* break it!" Ba Thet replied. "Be patient, my uncle. They are doing their best."

"And while they are doing that I shall drown," Sing Noi shouted bitterly. "Why don't *you* do something?"

Neither Ba Thet nor Chaung Thak had an answer to that. They had done all they could, and it had not been enough. This was the kind of situation neither had ever known before. Forty feet away Poo Koon was hidden, save for his trunk. Trapped under the rocks, Sing Noi was even worse threatened. If the water level rose another six or eight inches he would drown!

Tears welled slowly from Ba Thet's eyes and coursed down his dirty face. To sit helplessly by while his elephant and his uncle died was almost more than he could bear. Yet there was absolutely nothing he could do.

Even Sing Noi seemed to realize that shouting could not help, and fell silent. For several minutes no word passed among the three of them. Overhead a hornbill flapped heavily across the valley, little more than fifty feet above the water, his hoarse call drowned by the hiss of the falling rain.

Then above the sound of water came a different noise—a deep, startling *hurrrmmmph!*—and a terrific splashing. Two heads turned as if worked by some clockwork device. For a moment Ba Thet and Chaung Thak stared, their eyes bulging in astonishment. The last time they had looked that way they had seen only Poo Koon's trunk waving slowly backward and forward above the water. Now the head and part of his back were visible. He was floating in the pool—and struggling wildly to get out.

"He's free! He's free!" Ba Thet screeched, and tried to drag his hand out of the hole. Sing Noi's grip tightened, and held him prisoner.

"Who's free? What's happening?" Sing Noi yelled, hoping for news that he was going to be rescued.

"Poo Koon is free!" Ba Thet and Chaung Thak yelled the news together, while Ba Thet added, "Let go my hand, Uncle. Now we can do something for him." Sing Noi slowly released his grip on Ba Thet's hand. Even in his little prison he could hear the big tusker bellowing.

Poo Koon was threshing the water madly as he fought to get out of the pit. Like all elephants he was a natural swimmer. Nor was it a new thing for him to be entirely submerged and breathing through his trunk, held high above water.

More than once he had played a joke on Ba Thet and Sing Noi when they had been crossing a deeper than usual river. Instead of swimming he sometimes decided to walk on the bottom as soon as the water got deep enough. With his trunk up so that he could breathe, he allowed himself to drop until his feet were on the riverbed, then walked the rest of the way, giving his two riders an unexpected ducking.

Being trapped in the pit had been different, for his feet had been held in the mud. The moment he broke them free he had filled his huge lungs and floated to the surface. Now he was struggling to climb out of the pit, and beginning to panic when his forefeet could not get a firm grip on the slope Ba Thet and Chaung Thak had dug to help him.

There was little danger of his drowning, but there was a worse danger facing him. The panic fear that was making his heart thump wildly, combined with the tremendous struggle he was putting up, might easily cause him to have a sudden heart failure. He would not be the first elephant to die that way, and the two who rushed across to try and help him knew the danger only too well.

Chaung Thak forgot that he was an old man with a permanently aching leg. As he followed Ba Thet his limp disappeared for the time being. He helped lift the heavy dragging chain and carry it nearer Poo Koon.

"Poo Koon! Poo Koon!" Ba Thet was almost delirious with new-found hope and joy as he yelled to their tusker. They got as near to the edge of the pit as they dared and held out the loop in the chain, inviting the big tusker to slip his trunk through it and take a grip.

Poo Koon saw them clearly enough, but ignoring the chain, he made even greater efforts to scramble out. He lurched and wallowed, sometimes submerging as his feet slipped and he plunged forward and down again. Every moment his fear grew worse.

"*Hmit! Hmit!*" Ba Thet screamed. Then, remembering he did not want the tusker to kneel, he changed his command to one of "Stand still!" Poo Koon's eyes were rolling in fear, yet after Ba Thet had repeated his command several times more the sound of the familiar voice steadied the elephant.

"Take this. Come on, you old fool, take this!" Ba Thet shouted when it seemed as if Poo Koon was calming down a little. "Take the chain. Come on, come on!"

Poo Koon reached out, not to take the chain, but to lay the tip of his trunk on Ba Thet's shoulder. In that moment the big tusker needed comfort, and Ba Thet did something that always brought a little gurgle of pleasure from the elephant. He blew gently into Poo Koon's trunk.

It had a surprising effect. The rolling eyes steadied, and Poo Koon stopped his struggling. After a second or so Ba Thet repeated his command. "Come on, take the chain. Come on now," he coaxed. "Take the chain . . . and yooooo!"

Poo Koon curled the tip of his trunk through the loop in the chain and began to haul in the slack. Cleverly he coiled the slack around the thicker part of his trunk, watched in silence by Ba Thet and Chaung Thak.

"Are you ready?" Ba Thet asked. "All right. Come on now—yooooo!"

Poo Koon gave a little heave, and there was a crackling and chittering from the chain as links straightened under the strain. Then the big heave began. Poo Koon reached forward as far as he could, pulling himself until his chest was against the front of the pit; then he gave a mighty, continuous heave. It was the kind of effort he loved to make when he had to deal with a teak log that was bigger than usual.

Chaung Thak was not watching the elephant now. He had backed away a few yards and was watching the boulder on top of the rubble that held Sing Noi prisoner. It was a big boulder, and the chain had been fastened to it. However, Poo Koon was a big elephant. If his mighty heaving brought the boulder rolling off the top of the rubble, that would be the end. There would be nothing else to which they could anchor the chain.

Ba Thet was thinking only of Poo Koon. Slowly, while the chain seemed to dig into the thicker part of his trunk, the big tusker heaved himself up from the pit. His head was thrown back now as far as it would go.

The whole thing held in the balance. Poo Koon needed a fresh grip. He had hauled himself as far out of the pit as he could, and needed someone to help him get that little bit of extra hauling power. Ba Thet swung on the taut chain, in an effort to give the tusker the pull he needed.

Then from the pile of rocks came a wailing cry from Sing Noi. The boulder was seven or eight feet above the older man, and the tremendous pull on it was making it rock to and fro. It was threatening to move out of the little depression its weight had dug in the debris. If that happened it would come rolling off the top.

Sing Noi was not afraid of that. What was terrifying him now was the fact that the movement of the boulder was disturbing the smaller rocks above him and sending showers of wet earth and small stones onto him. He could feel the whole mass of debris quivering, and was afraid the rocks above him were going to slip down and crush him to death.

Chaung Thak rushed over to see what was wrong with his old friend, but before he could reach him there was a grumbling and grinding of rock on rock, and the key boulder moved.

As it slid forward it allowed Poo Koon to slide back. His forefeet, which had got their first grip on the surface of the river mud, slipped off. Down went the elephant into the pit again, and as the dragging chain tightened it pulled the boulder over the lip. Weighing several tons, it crunched over the tiny hollow in which it had been sitting and rolled ponderously down the heap of debris.

Ba Thet shrieked and jumped for his life, but the boulder stopped yards from him and came to rest in the water to one side of the flooded pit.

Poo Koon bellowed in shocked surprise, and Ba Thet turned to see what had happened. His spirits sank as he realized what it all meant. They had been so near to success. Now they were worse off than ever, for the boulder that had been the anchor on which Poo Koon had pulled was no use in its present position.

Chaung Thak shook his head sadly as he walked toward Ba Thet. The old man's shoulders were sagging, and his limp had come back. Laying a hand on Ba Thet's shoulder, he said gently, "Let us go back to camp. The jungle spirits are too strong for us. They have decided to take Poo Koon and your uncle. Let us go, for it will be a terrible thing to stay and watch them die. If there was anything we could do, I would stay but we can do nothing. Come, Ba Thet, take an old man's advice, come back to camp."

"No!" Ba Thet shouted fiercely. "We *can* do something. We *must* do something."

"Come with me," Chaung Thak pleaded, and when Ba Thet angrily pushed the comforting hand off his shoulder, the older man turned and began to walk downstream.

Ba Thet, the Undefeated

CHAUNG THAK HAD PLODDED ABOUT THIRTY YARDS WHEN Ba Thet came splashing after him. There was a brightness about the boy's eyes, which might have been unshed tears, or some new spirit giving him fresh strength. He halted Chaung Thak and swung him around until he faced upstream again.

"Four years I have known you," Ba Thet shouted. "I came with my uncle the first season when we began buying Poo Koon. I was twelve years old, and everyone in the camp spoke of you as a great man. They told me you had been the best *oozie* ever to ride a tusker. You were a man of wisdom, a man of great courage. You feared nothing."

"I cannot help what men said of me," Chaung Thak replied. "Why do you say these things to me now?"

"Because they were lies," was the fierce reply. "You are neither a man of wisdom nor a brave man. What do you think men will say when they know that you left me—a young *paijaik*—to stay with Sing Noi until he died. What will they say when I tell them that if you had stayed we could have saved both Poo Koon *and* my uncle? They will turn aside, and the old women in the villages will shake their heads and know that you have become a *very old man*, with no courage at all."

At that Chaung Thak slapped Ba Thet across the face so hard that the boy quivered.

"If you were not a very old man." Ba Thet snapped, "I would throw you into the mud for that, but I won't do it. You are just a poor, feeble old man. I feel sorry for you." And turning on his heel he began to trot upstream, throwing showers of dirty spray all about him.

Chaung Thak stared after him. Slowly the sagging shoulders straightened. Slowly the despair faded from his eyes, to give place to a gleam of anger. Suddenly he began to trot after Ba Thet. He was limping a little, but trotting just the same. He got back to where they had left the elephant in time to see Ba Thet beginning to free the chain from the boulder.

"Why do this?" Chaung Thak asked harshly.

"Because there are four dragging chains and four wire ropes," Ba Thet snapped. "I shall fasten them together, carry one end up the bank, and fasten it around some of the trees. It shall never be said that *I* sat down and let them die."

"You are a fool, and it will not work," Chaung

131

Thak said grimly, but he began to help loosen the chain. In ten frantic minutes they fastened four sets of dragging chains and wires together. They carried one end up the bank and secured it around four trees growing at the foot of the hill. Then Ba Thet scrambled down the bank once more and for the second time in half an hour held out the chain loop to Poo Koon.

Chaung Thak reached him as the big tusker began to draw in the slack.

"The chain should be tightened," Chaung Thak said coldly. "Perhaps even a very old man can show you something."

He did. He showed Ba Thet how to take in slack so that the chain was almost taut when Poo Koon slipped his trunk through the loop and prepared for what must be his last fight for life. There was a dullness about his eyes now, showing that his great strength was waning.

"Is everything ready?" Ba Thet finally asked. When Chaung Thak nodded, the boy turned to Poo Koon and in a quiet voice said, "Now, if you want to work again for me and my uncle, you must pull as you have never pulled before. Are you ready? *Yooooo—yooooo!*"

Poo Koon pulled. From somewhere in his huge body he summoned up new strength. Again the wire ropes thrummed and the chain links made a chittering sound. Once more Poo Koon began to heave himself out of the pit.

"Come on, come on," Chaung Thak roared. "Onto the rope. Swing down with all your strength. Swing. . . . *Swing!*"

They swung on the tight wire rope, giving a little extra pull to Poo Koon. They could contribute only a little, but it turned the tide. The big tusker's head was thrown back as far as it would go, and when the old man and the sixteen-year-old youth swung on the rope, it did the trick.

Poo Koon found a foothold with his right foot. He gave a mighty gurgling roar. Muddy water splashed around in fountains, covering man and boy. Then there was an even mightier splash, and a second later Ba Thet and Chaung Thak were sprawled in the water as the wire rope suddenly went slack. Poo Koon was out of the pit!

Several seconds passed before Ba Thet could find the strength to get to his knees. When he dared look he saw a great gray-black mound. It was their tusker. He had heaved himself free, and now lay on his side, more exhausted than either Ba Thet or Chaung Thak.

Ba Thet splashed across to him on his hands and knees. He laid his wet cheek against the tusker's head, and after a moment or so drummed gently with the knuckles of his right hand on Poo Koon's forehead. It was a thing he often did when they had been bathing in the river, and it always gave so much pleasure to the huge beast that he would swing

133

his trunk around and gently rub the tip along Ba
Thet's back.

He did not do that now, but he did make a low
gurgling noise deep in his throat to show his grati-
tude.

"You old . . . fool. You old fool!" Ba Thet said
chokily. They were not the sort of words he wanted
to use. But they were the only ones that came to

his mind. The tusker was too big to be hugged, yet that was what Ba Thet wanted to do at that moment.

He could feel the huge body trembling. The battle had been a hard one, and it would be a few minutes before Poo Koon's straining lungs got all the air they needed. Later there would have to be some doctoring to the trunk, for the chain had bitten into the soft skin.

It was Chaung Thak who shattered Ba Thet's overwhelming joy and relief. The old man was trembling even more than the tusker as he crawled over to place a hand on Ba Thet's back and gasp out, "You have saved him. Now what about your uncle? Is Sing Noi to die? Or have you a plan to save him?"

Without waiting for a reply, he turned and limped wearily down to the crevice in the pile of rocks where he could speak to Sing Noi. The river was still rising, and there had been no sound from the prisoner for some time.

"Sing Noi!" Chaung Thak called. "How are you, my old friend? We have freed the tusker."

"I—am—drowning!" came the slow, labored reply. "The water will be up to my lips in a minute or so. Good-bye, Chaung Thak. Good-bye."

But Ba Thet refused to believe it was the end for his uncle. They had rescued Poo Koon, and they would do the same for Sing Noi. In the next few minutes he achieved something like a miracle. Even Chaung Thak, with his vast experience of elephants, was amazed when the big tusker was finally persuaded to heave his huge bulk out of the muddy water.

When Bill Johnson came around the bend of the river to bring the bad news that they could not break the logjam, he saw something that stopped him in his tracks. The unbelievable had happened. Not only was Poo Koon out of the pit, but he was perched a third of the way up the pile of rocks and debris.

The tusker was standing almost upright. His hind legs bore his great weight while he used his front feet as a balance. His massive forehead pushed up at the end of the teak log that had caused the breakdown of the riverbank.

It was a spectacle Bill Johnson would surely remember for many years. Without a doubt, whenever men talked about wonderful elephants, the teak wallah would think of Poo Koon. What he was seeing now was magnificent, and crazily dangerous. If the tusker slipped he would certainly kill himself.

Forgetting his weariness of a moment earlier, Bill Johnson began to run. The last time he had seen Poo Koon the big bull had been crazed with pain and filled with a desire to kill or maim anyone who came near him. Now he was straining every nerve and sinew to raise the log.

Below Poo Koon, Ba Thet and Chaung Thak each

had an arm in the cleft in the rocks, beyond which lay Sing Noi. Both of them screamed encouragement to the tusker, urging him, imploring him to give one more heave upward.

The first upward push on the teak log had taken a great strain off the rocks imprisoning Sing Noi, and he had been able to lift his head out of the water. Now Ba Thet and Chaung Thak waited for the rocks to move a little more and enable them to drag the prisoner out.

The log that Poo Koon was trying so hard to lift needed to be pushed up at least another six inches, thus taking the weight off a stone that was partially blocking the gap through which Sing Noi would have to be dragged to freedom.

Bill Johnson saw what was needed and, yelling to the men who had followed him, scrambled up onto the pile, and when the others had reached him they heaved together in an effort to move the teak log higher.

It was a vain effort, and they did not waste more than a minute on it. They turned their attention to some small rocks lying on the teak log and bundled them off the pile, but still the tusker could not heave the log the necessary few inches more.

Then Chaung Thak called to Poo Koon to climb higher up the pile. If he could do that, moving the log upward would be easier.

Johnson looked down at the tusker, then ordered

his men off the mass of rocks and rubble. He followed them, and stood watching while Poo Koon did something that would have made any circus trainer of elephants envious. The big tusker began to feel for a foothold some eight or nine inches above where he was now standing. It involved balancing for a moment or so on one leg.

Ba Thet and Chaung Thak waited anxiously for a chance to pull the awkward piece of rock out of the crevice, thus widening the gap sufficiently for them to drag Sing Noi to freedom. They were kneeling, waist deep, and Sing Noi's face was only just clear of the water. It had been a desperately close thing when Poo Koon first lifted the log and gave them a little time.

Bill Johnson stood open-mouthed as he watched Poo Koon ease one foot upward onto a stone, which seemed certain to roll once it had any weight on it. Yet the big tusker had judged his foothold correctly. The stone did not roll. A few moments later the other hind foot went up.

Poo Koon gave a half-hearted roar, as if asking them all to see what he had done; then he heaved upward with his forehead. Ba Thet and Chaung Thak saw a tiny gap appear above the stone at which they were tugging. The weight was off it and a second later they had the stone out.

"Get him out . . . get him out!" Bill Johnson roared, for Poo Koon had begun to waver. That final heave had not only taken all his strength, but it had broken his balance.

Ba Thet and Chaung Thak heaved, and there was a squeal of pain from Sing Noi as they dragged him out into the open, scraping skin off his elbows and thighs in the process. A moment later Bill Johnson was reaching down to grab the rescuers. He dragged them backward, and since they were still hanging on to Sing Noi he, too, was pulled clear. Johnson did not stop until he had dragged them a dozen yards away. Then they all looked up in time to see the end of the drama.

Poo Koon's last mighty thrust upward had made the rescue of Sing Noi possible, but it had cost the big tusker his balance. He had broken the teak log free from the rocks in which it had been buried, and with nothing against his forehead to steady him, Poo Koon began to fall.

He gave a trumpet blast of dismay as he tried to turn sideways—perhaps with the intention of stepping down off the rocks. The distance was a little more than five feet, too far for such a heavy animal.

Poo Koon's trunk grabbed at a rock and brought it away out of the pile; then he rolled down the slope and, raising a terrific sheet of brown spray as he hit the water, came to rest in the mud of the riverbed.

Chaung Thak, the Wise

BILL JOHNSON BEGAN TO ROAR OUT ORDERS. THE *oozies* were to bring up the elephants. Another man was to rush back to camp and tell four more *oozies* to bring their elephants. They were also to bring spare chestbands—the broad, woven straps that take the strain when an elephant is hauling logs.

Ba Thet was kneeling by his uncle, but Sing Noi lifted himself a little, saw their tusker lying a few yards away, and said, "Go to him, nephew. I shall not die, but Poo Koon may, if he lies there without a struggle. Tell him he has to fight to get up. He is our tusker, Ba Thet. We've got to save him."

Ba Thet hurried over to Poo Koon and knelt by his head. The tusker's eyes were open, but he was making no movement of any kind. That could be fatal, especially after a fall. If an elephant lay too long, death was almost certain. For the most part they even slept standing up.

If Bill Johnson had felt tired and despondent earlier, he showed no sign of it now. He went over to Sing Noi, shook hands with him, and told him how delighted he was they had been able to rescue him. "We'll soon get you up on the bank. Some of the men are coming and they can take you to camp."

"Mr. Johnson, I would like to stay with our elephant," Sing Noi pleaded. "He needs me now."

Johnson's answer to that was to lift Sing Noi and carry him over to where Ba Thet was talking to Poo Koon. Sing Noi huddled by the tusker's head and began talking to him.

"Will he die?" Ba Thet asked anxiously.

"No!" the older man said angrily. "If he were without courage he might lie here until death came, but he is not a coward. Poo Koon, you are to stand up. *Tah! Tah!*" But the big tusker merely rolled his eyes a little at the repeated command. For the moment he could not stand up.

"We shall not leave you, you old fool," Ba Thet crooned, and he drummed gently with his knuckles on the tusker's broad forehead.

Just before the extra tuskers arrived there was a loud report from somewhere downstream. Bill Johnson looked around, then gave a grunt. "Hm! Yes, you would go when our trouble is almost over."

The roar was made by the logjam, which had finally broken up of its own accord. The accumulation of water behind the mass of hard-packed logs had proved too great. The key log had snapped, and within seconds the whole mass was on the move. The report was made by the hundreds of tons of logs and the many thousands of tons of water as they suddenly surged downstream in a chaotic flood that would bring most of the teak to the mainstream without much delay.

With the logjam broken, the water drained down very quickly, and soon Poo Koon was lying on wet mud, with the nearest water some yards away. The *oozies* dug a channel under the tusker and passed three of the broad breastbands under him.

The three bands were then equally spaced under Poo Koon's ribs and the six tuskers divided into two teams. With three elephants on each side hauling on the breastbands, they managed, after one or two slight mishaps, to haul Poo Koon upright.

He was shaky, and refused to put one of his hind feet onto the mud. Bill Johnson shot a quick glance at Ba Thet, but made no comment. With three elephants on each side of him and the broad breastbands supporting him underneath, Poo Koon was slowly moved downstream.

It was almost night by the time they got back to the camp, and by then a change for the worse was coming over the "patient." He was beginning to roar peevishly, and had already made one jab at a helper with his undamaged tusk.

Chaung Thak diagnosed the trouble. Going over to Bill Johnson, he said quietly, "Mr. Johnson, it is his tusk that hurts. He needs to be given more opium."

"Some *more* opium!" Bill Johnson said sharply. "What do you mean *more?* Has he already been given opium?"

"Yes, sir," Chaung Thak said smoothly. "That is how we were able to get him out of the pit. We had to."

"Never mind that now. I'll hear the story later. Who has the opium?"

"Have you got any of the opium left?" Chaung Thak asked Ba Thet. "If you do, give it to Mr. Johnson."

Bill Johnson's eyes narrowed as Ba Thet brought out from his shorts' pocket a sticky ball of brown stuff, which gave off the unmistakable smell that goes with opium.

"It is from the packages left under the rocks," Ba Thet explained. "I gave some to Poo Koon—and it quieted him."

"Give him some more now," Bill Johnson ordered.

The old man and Ba Thet went over to the kitchen. Ba Thet was worrying about how to get Poo Koon to take the opium. But Chaung Thak had remembered that he had not had time to clean out his rice pans. He had filled them with water to keep the rice soft, and now, after draining the water away,

144

he had sufficient rice to make a nice-sized ball. They put the opium in the middle, after mixing salt with the rice to make it tasty.

Poo Koon grunted angrily, but took the tidbit. For a moment it seemed as if he would spit it out, but Chaung Thak had mixed just enough salt with the pill to hide the taste of opium, and to the relief of everyone, Poo Koon swallowed it.

All hands were called to help build a "crush" in which Poo Koon could be held while Bill Johnson operated on him. The crush was a simple but strong, compound just large enough to hold an elephant. One end was blocked by a tree chosen for its uprightness and its strength. On each side of the tree they built a fence about twelve feet long. The open end could be closed by tying strong bamboo poles across the twin fencing.

With everyone working hard, the crush was completed in an hour, and Poo Koon, still under the influence of the opium, went in quietly enough. The heavy bamboo poles were fastened in place behind him, and he was a prisoner.

Bill Johnson's surgical implements were simple enough. He had a short saw and a file. Standing on a ladder leaning against the tree, he began to saw the jagged end of Poo Koon's tusk, while the *oozies* and *paijaiks* watched in breathless silence. They had seen Johnson do this operation before, but in the past it had usually been to shorten tusks that had grown too long or too sharp. They had never seen a broken tusk operated on.

The opium must have dulled Poo Koon's senses completely, for he allowed Bill Johnson to work without raising any objection at all. Even when the exposed nerve was extracted the tusker did no more than grunt.

Trimming the end of the saw cut with the file, Johnson then soaked a wad of cotton in antiseptic and opium and pushed it gently into the nerve cavity. The operation was over.

Sing Noi and Ba Thet went to talk soothingly to Poo Koon, and even gave him a generous tidbit of salted rice cake, but got no response. For the time being the tusker was completely under the influence of the drug.

Throughout the night there was no rest for anyone. The shattered camp had to be rebuilt. First up was a shelter for Sing Noi so that he could rest out of the incessant rain. Then they built a cooking shelter to enable Chaung Thak to prepare one of the biggest meals ever eaten in the camp.

An hour before dawn the rain stopped, as suddenly as if someone had turned off a tap. The last pieces of atap roofing went up, and the whole camp lay down to rest.

The next day Bill Johnson sent the men out at

noon, for they had to get the teak logs downriver to the Bangkok mills. If they missed the floods that the monsoon rains brought, the logs would have to lie about for another year.

Ba Thet was excused from work, since there was no elephant for him to ride. Sing Noi was still sleeping, and Poo Koon, still in the crush, seemed content to doze. He stood on three legs, supported by the bands under his ribs.

Ba Thet tried to see what was the matter with the left hind foot, but the moment he laid a hand on it, no matter how gently he did it, there was a rumbling grunt of pain.

For three days men and elephants worked every hour of daylight, for there were more monsoon storms, more rises of the river, and more logs to be helped out and downstream.

Then came the day when the season ended. All the logs had floated downstream and the government official had arrived with the pay money. He came with an armed guard of Thai police in their dark-blue uniforms. The money was in shining ticals.

A table was set up under an awning in front of Bill Johnson's tent, because for the moment the rain had stopped and the sun was shining strongly. On the table were two books. One contained Johnson's accounts, showing exactly how much was owing to each man and boy and how much was to be paid for the hiring of the elephants. The second book was the receipt book. Since none of the teak men could write, they "signed" for their pay by pressing a thumb on an inked pad, then putting the thumbprint in a space alongside the sum of money paid to them. Once they had "signed" that was the end of it. The thumbprint was there to show that they had got their money.

Sing Noi went up to the table when his name was called, and made a little sign of respect to Bill Johnson. Johnson told him the sum owed to him, counted it out in little piles of ten, then pushed the receipt book over so that Sing Noi could put his thumbprint in the right place.

Bill Johnson was frowning as he watched the older man scrape the piles of coins into a bag he had brought for that purpose. "You will notice, Sing Noi," he said, "that there is no retaining fee for next season."

"I had noticed that, Mr. Johnson," Sing Noi said. And in an anxious voice he asked, "Has my work not been good that you do not want me for next time?"

"Your work has been very good," was the prompt reply. "I am worried about your elephant—his hind foot. It is not improving. I think perhaps a bone is broken. If there is. . . ." He did not finish the sentence, but shook his head sadly.

"Perhaps it will be better when he has had a good rest," Sing Noi suggested hopefully.

"I hope it will," Johnson said, but added, "In the

meantime, I cannot offer you a work contract for next season—unless you get another elephant. I am afraid that Poo Koon will never haul logs again. Some days have passed since he hurt his leg, and it shows no sign of going right. I have tried to examine it several times, but he will not put it on the ground. I am sorry."

"Will there be compensation?" Sing Noi asked anxiously. "In the contract does it not say that when an elephant is badly injured while working for the—"

"I'm sorry, Sing Noi," Bill Johnson interrupted, shooting a sideways glance at the Thai government official sitting by his table. "If it were *my* teak company there would certainly be compensation. I have spoken to the government paymaster who sits by my side, but he says it is impossible to pay anything in compensation. The reason is a simple one: when Poo Koon was hurt he was not working for the teak company."

There was a low murmur of disgust from the listening *oozies,* most of whom owned their own elephants. Bill Johnson nodded, saying, "I know how you feel. *I* feel the same way. I think Poo Koon earned compensation—but the government rules say not.

Sing Noi gave another little salutation, and was moving away when he was called back. "There is something else," Bill Johnson said. Dropping his hand down to the ground by his chair, he drew up a sealed bag and let it fall heavily on the table in front of him. There was the unmistakable chink of coins.

"This may console you a little, Sing Noi," he said. Looking at the assembled men and boys, he added, "You probably all know the law about smuggled opium. For those who help the police, either by giving information about smugglers or actually handing in smuggled opium, there is a reward.

The scowls vanished from the faces of the half circle of men and boys. Even Sing Noi and his nephew Ba Thet suddenly looked interested.

"There were four packages of opium left under the fall of rocks at the riverbank," Bill Johnson said. With a little grin he added, "One package was opened, but we won't say anything about that. It was opened for a very good purpose. Anyway, the reward is half the value of the opium, and it is here in this bag. It may help you buy another elephant, Sing Noi."

Sing Noi's face was wreathed in smiles as he stepped forward to "sign" for the reward. As he stepped back Bill Johnson called Chaung Thak's name, although the cook had already been paid.

"When the missionary doctor came to see whether I was still alive," Johnson said, chuckling, "he told me that 'someone' had sent word that there was a party of Mooser tribesmen heading south with an oxcart laden with opium. As you know the doctor's journey wasn't necessary since I had more or less recovered by the time he arrived, but he did tell me he had managed to pass word on to the police. This is the result." He lifted a second bag onto the table. "You are a man who can kill two birds with one stone, aren't you, Chaung Thak?"

Chaung Thak looked as puzzled as all the others, and Johnson laughed as he explained. "It means that you are clever enough to be able to do two things at one and the same time. You sent for the missionary doctor and you sent word about opium."

"I am always anxious to help the police," Chaung Thak murmured, but there was a twinkle in his eyes.

"The Mooser men were caught, the opium confiscated," Bill Johnson said. "So, of course, there is a reward. It has been decided that half the reward shall go to the missionary doctor. I imagine he will spend the money on drugs and bandages for when we get hurt. The other half will be divided between you and the two *oozies* who carried the message to the doctor. Sign here."

Chaung Thak placed his thumbmark on the sheet, and when he carried the bag of ticals away he was accompanied by the two young *oozies* who were to share the reward with him.

That night, when the fires had burned to a dying red glow and the silence was so great that the distant *pyoo-pyoo-pyoo* call of a porcupine was so clear it seemed to be only just outside the camp, there was a rustle at the doorway of the shelter where Ba Thet and his uncle were sleeping.

Ba Thet woke and grasped his knife. Thefts after a teak-camp payday were not unknown, and there was a worthwhile hoard of ticals in the hole Sing Noi had dug under where his sleeping mat was laid. Sing Noi sat up, but a moment later uncle and nephew relaxed as they heard a whisper from outside. It was Chaung Thak.

"Light no lamp," he cautioned when given permission to enter. "I have come to ask you to help me help you."

"Help you to help us!" Sing Noi whispered, perplexed. "What do you mean?"

"Thy nephew, old friend," Chaung Thak said, with the merest hint of a chuckle in his voice, "accused me some days ago of being a man without courage, and of being also a very *old* man, and a man without wisdom. Is that true, Ba Thet?"

"It is true," Ba Thet admitted. "I meant later to say that I was sorry I had said such a thing, for you proved that you did have courage."

"I have come to prove that I am also a man of wisdom," Chaung Thak said. "Sing Noi, you know that I have worked with elephants since the time when I was far smaller than thy nephew here."

"That is true," Sing Noi agreed. "But what is all this about?"

"I am going to make Poo Koon's leg right," was the astonishing answer. "I kept some opium, Ba Thet, and there is enough to make Poo Koon quiet. Give it to him, and when it has had an effect, I shall show you something even a clever young *paijaik* may not know." His grin took the sting out of his words, and he held out a tidbit for Poo Koon.

Ba Thet took the ball of rice and salt that Chaung Thak had brought with him and hid the opium in the middle. A few minutes later Poo Koon had swallowed it.

Half an hour later, when even the cook's fire had died down to gray ash, the two men and Ba Thet crept out and went back to the crush where Poo Koon was still standing on three legs, his weight partially supported by the chestbands running from side to side of the crush.

Chaung Thak got his two helpers to aid him in lifting the injured foot as far from the ground as possible. Then they lashed it to one of the side supports of the crush. Poo Koon could not put it down no matter how hard he tried. He was beginning to make little grumbling noises, a fact that made Ba Thet nervous.

A broad band was fastened around the bottom of Poo Koon's foot. Attached to the band were three short lengths of rope. When they were all in place Chaung Thak wiped beads of perspiration from his forehead and whispered, "What we are going to do now is to take a rope end each and, when I give the word, jerk down on it as hard as we can. Put all your strength and weight onto it. Is that clear?"

"You are mad, Chaung Thak," Sing Noi whispered. "The pain will make Poo Koon go crazy. He could kill all three of us."

"Ba Thet, is it possible that thy uncle is short of courage?" Chaung Thak asked jokingly, adding in the same breath, "But I know he is a brave man and understands elephants. However, we gave Poo Koon opium so he will not feel the pain."

"But why do we do this?" Sing Noi asked anxiously. "Can pulling down on Poo Koon's foot mend a broken bone?"

"If I am guessing right, old friend," Chaung Thak said soberly, "there is no broken bone—only a foot that has been driven up hard and something pushed out of place. If we can pull down hard on the foot, then I hope we shall put back into place whatever he displaced when he fell so heavily."

Soberly Ba Thet and his uncle each took a rope end. Chaung Thak took the third rope. He was actually kneeling under Poo Koon's head, a dangerous place if the tusker should feel any real pain.

At a word from Chaung Thak all three swung their weight down on the ropes as heavily as they could. Poo Koon grunted and that was all.

"Again," Chaung Thak said, and now he seemed less sure of himself. "It will maybe need a few pulls.

An elephant's foot is strong—very strong."

At a grunt from Chaung Thak, Ba Thet and Sing Noi swung their weight down again on Poo Koon's foot. This time there was an audible, hard *click*, and from Poo Koon came what sounded like a long deep sigh.

"Again?" Sing Noi asked, but Chaung Thak shook his head.

"No, I think we have done it," he said happily. "Did you hear the *click?* That was when something that had been jarred out of place went back into its right place. I will untie the tusker's leg and we'll see what he does."

He untied the bonds holding Poo Koon's foot off the ground, and after a moment the tusker slowly lowered his foot. He seemed to be testing it, putting just a little of his weight on it. A moment later the end of his trunk swung around and nuzzled the back of Chaung Thak's neck. The old man gave a squeak of alarm. But when Ba Thet moved nearer, the trunk tip came to his back and snuffled his neck. Poo Koon then wrapped his trunk around Ba Thet and carefully lifted him up onto his neck. Though he was heavily doped by opium he knew that something good had happened to his injured foot, and he was showing his pleasure.

Next morning the *oozies* and the *paijaiks* were preparing to move off to their respective villages. Many of them would not meet again until the beginning of the next teak season. Chaung Thak was packing Bill Johnson's kit, because the teak wallah was going on vacation before beginning other duties dealing with the logs now moving along the main river to Bangkok.

"Mr. Johnson, there is someone to speak to you," Chaung Thak called. "An *oozie* named Sing Noi."

Bill Johnson looked up and sighed. He was sorry for Sing Noi, but there was nothing he could do for him. He walked to the tent door.

Then he stopped. Standing a few yards away was the great bull, the big tusker Poo Koon. Sitting on his neck was Ba Thet, while half leaning on the tusker's trunk was Sing Noi, his face glowing with a smile of happiness.

"Mr. Johnson," Sing Noi said, "I would like to sign the paper to come and work for you next season. There is a small fee to pay, if you remember."

Bill Johnson's eyes narrowed. Realizing what he was thinking, Ba Thet scraped a big toenail gently behind one of Poo Koon's ears and ordered him to march. Almost as if he knew he was being shown off, Poo Koon sedately marched around in a circle, came back, knelt, stood up, then knelt again.

"Who worked the miracle?" Bill Johnson asked, and added, "Oh," when Ba Thet and his uncle indicated Chaung Thak.

"I have—a little knowledge of elephants, sir," the old man said, the corners of his mouth twitching as

he tried to control a grin of delight. "A little opium to quiet Poo Koon—a little help from my old friend Sing Noi and his nephew—I hoped it would make the foot right. And it did."

"You are a clever old rogue, Chaung Thak, and I'm glad you are on my side," Bill Johnson said, laughing. He went into the tent, and in minutes the agreement was signed for the next season and the retaining fee handed over.

"Good luck," Johnson said as he clapped Poo Koon on the trunk. Then he turned and went back to his tent.

Sing Noi handed over the retaining fee to Chaung Thak.

"A gift to thy wife, my friend," he said. "Tell her from me that she has a very clever husband."

"Clever?" Chaung Thak asked, his eyebrows raised as he looked straight at Ba Thet.

Ba Thet nodded, grinned, then said, "I know I was wrong, Chaung Thak. You are brave and you are wise—though maybe you are a *little* old."

Then he touched Poo Koon behind the ear and the big tusker moved off. Poo Koon would spend the next three months roaming the jungle country near the village where his two masters lived, and the slight ache left in his foot where a sinew had been badly misplaced would by then have faded even beyond an elephant's memory.